# Hank Winton

## SMOKECHASER

*By the same author*

**SKI PATROL**

# HANK WINTON

## SMOKECHASER

By Montgomery M. Atwater

Illustrated by E. Joseph Dreany

RANDOM HOUSE   NEW YORK

TO MY SON

*James Engen Atwater*

WHO MAY SOME DAY
BE A SMOKECHASER
HIMSELF

TWELFTH PRINTING

PUBLISHED IN NEW YORK BY RANDOM HOUSE, INC.

AND SIMULTANEOUSLY IN TORONTO, CANADA BY

RANDOM HOUSE OF CANADA, LTD. 1947.

MANUFACTURED IN THE U.S.A.

# CONTENTS

# CONTENTS

# ILLUSTRATIONS

# O N E

Springtime in the Rockies

"When it's springtime in the Rockies
I am coming back to you,
To the old Three Rivers District
With her bonny skies of blue."

BAWLED at the wilderness with more power than
harmony, this ditty roused a pine squirrel to fretful
chattering. In a patch of aspen near the river an elk
raised his head from the tender young buds and
galumphed away, leaving rags of winter coat on every
twig. A beaver traveling upstream from eddy to eddy
on the spring migration of his kind slapped the water
with his rubbery tail. And far up on the mountain-
side a coyote, drifting along as lightly as a puff of
smoke, put into a single protesting bark all his contempt for the peculiar ways of men.

"Enthusiastic audience," grumbled Forest Ranger
James H. Crawford. "Maybe they'll like the second

verse better." He filled his chest with the sharp mountain air and threw back his head.

"But the skies aren't blue," hastily pointed out John Stemple, alternate ranger of the Three Rivers District. His rare and winning smile lit his serious young face as he huddled against the leeward side of a thick spruce. Both of them were soaked and shivering from the spring blizzard which had caught them on the trail. There was no reason at all for their obvious good humor.

"Ah, you too," snarled the ranger in mock rage. "And do you, with the silly grin on your puss, realize that in the million acres of primitive wilderness which surround us, not to mention an equal amount of half-melted snow, I represent the majesty and power of the United States Forest Service?" Towering a foot and a half over his companion, his long arms making eloquent gestures, his sodden hat dripping water down his neck, the ranger was a picture of bedraggled dignity.

Stemple laughed aloud. "Honestly, boss," he said, "sometimes you astound me. You act like a kid on the last day of school. You couldn't wait for the trail crew to rebuild twenty feet of cribwork and come up here like a sensible person. You had to light out afoot, with your pack on your back, just to get into the middle of your wilderness a day sooner. And now look at you."

Besides being two heads taller, the ranger was also enough older than Stemple to be his father. And ordinarily, an alternate does not tell the district ranger that he is acting "like a kid on the last day of school." But neither the people nor the circumstances were ordinary. Crawford and Stemple owed each other so much, had gone through so much together and understood each other so well, that there could be no question of formality between them. They were that unbeatable team: two men who trust each other completely. Besides that, they were alone, sixty miles from a highway or a town, ten miles from another human being or a house. They could not have been more completely on their own if they had been on a raft in the middle of the ocean. And they were enjoying every minute of it, including the storm. The time would come soon enough when they were heavily burdened with the thousand details of guarding this vast and priceless treasure of trees and grass and water and animals from fire. They relaxed now, while they could.

A grin split the face of the ranger, a face so weather-darkened that a winter cooped up in an office could only lighten the tan one or two shades. "Has anyone been stalking you for three months, trying to shackle a desk job on you?" he asked. "Not much. You've been out cruising timber and making snow surveys and range inspections, just having a great old time for yourself. Boy, you just don't know how close I came to getting stuck on the fire desk at Regional HQ."

"I guessed, though," replied John Stemple soberly. "It's bound to come too, if not this year, then next year, or the one after. What'll you do then?"

"I'll die," said Crawford flatly. "When you've been in the mountains as long as I have, it would be like hitching that elk to an ash wagon. . . . Well, let's pound a little trail."

The two shrugged into their packs, making faces as the loads pressed cold, wet cloth against their shoulders. The ranger led off, his long legs eating up the ground, yet Stemple with his shorter, quicker stride seemed to have no trouble keeping up. Both traveled at the loose-jointed, high-kneed trail gait of the woodsman which looks so casual but which devours trail uphill and down at a steady three miles per hour.

This, the mainline trail of the Three Rivers District, followed the side of the canyon which had most exposure to the sun. Timber lay in scattered groves connected by alpine parks and enormous, grassy hillsides. Soon the two foresters left the grove where they had taken shelter from the storm and began a long climb along the flank of a mountain. At almost the same instant the last of the storm whooped on down the canyon and the sun came out. It warmed the pussywillows, the buds swelling on the bare arms of aspen and cottonwood and the tender green stalk at the tip of each evergreen. It shone upon such a glory of wildflowers that the hillsides looked as if some unearthly artist had painted them with rainbows.

The opposite side of the canyon, black with its unbroken mantle of forest, presented a different picture. There, sheltered from the sun, the snow still lay in drifts three feet deep. Frost rising stubbornly out of the ground made a carpet of ice crystals, and in late afternoon avalanches thundered down from the cliffs above. In this high mountain wilderness the seasons were at war, and the two foresters picked their way across it as across a battlefield.

Even on the sunny side of the canyon there were steep gullies packed to the brim with the snow and wreckage of earlier avalanches. Presently Crawford and Stemple came to one. The trail disappeared into the snow and appeared again several hundred feet away. A stranger might have thought that the drift was only a shallow crust. But every fold and turn of the canyon was familiar to the ranger and his alternate, and they knew that the snow pack was at least fifty feet deep.

John edged out on it stamping hard with his caulked boots. Beneath a layer of slush he found the snow hard as concrete. He began to walk across.

"Now who's in a hurry?" The ranger's voice stopped him. "You know better than that."

Sheepishly, John returned to the edge of the snowbank and took the pole Crawford had been trimming. He started across again. The surface of the avalanche was tilted at a wicked angle and John walked on the edges of his boots, one careful step after another. Far below him boiled the Wolf River, glutted with melted snow and cakes of ice. Oddly, he did not use the pole to aid his footing, but held it across his body like a man on a tightrope. Crawford watched, swinging his hand axe nervously.

At the center of the avalanche, John seemed suddenly to lose his balance. He staggered, one leg sank knee-deep into the snow and he wrenched at it. Then, like magic, a black hole gaped in the white expanse with John in the middle of it, suspended on his pole. Up out of the depths rushed a chill breeze and the thunder of falling water.

"All right, Johnny," called the ranger. "I'll be right with you." With one tremendous sweep of the arm, he drove his axe through the four-inch butt of another pole, caught it as it fell and rushed out onto the avalanche.

In falling, John had turned almost all the way around. He was balanced chest-high on his crossbar and his face, turned toward the ranger, was calm. But his gray eyes looked almost black and there were beads of sweat on his forehead.

"Stay away from me, boss," he said quietly. "This thing is caving in more all the time. Stay away from me."

Crawford paid no attention to the warning. He could see as well as Stemple that the hole in the avalanche was growing. The pole on which John was hanging had a purchase of only a few inches at each end. The one the ranger carried was almost twice as long. He threw it now like a javelin and saw it land safely, bridging the chasm. Stemple immediately transferred his hold and began to edge his way along it toward safety. In a few seconds he was within reach of Crawford's long arms and the ranger took him by the jacket collar and dragged him bodily onto solid snow.

Five minutes was the measure of the adventure in time. Stemple said, "Thanks, boss. That glacier water is awfully cold, they tell me."

"That old man of the mountains really swings from his heels," replied the ranger.

And that was their measure of an accident which had come within a split second of costing at least one of them his life. But it was not bravado. They merely accepted the fact that the wilderness is like a playful giant who may crush a small thing like a man without even knowing it.

Delaying only long enough to cut another safety pole apiece, they marched out onto the avalanche again and this time found solid footing. On the far side they unslung their packs and rested.

For several minutes not a word was spoken. Their bodies relaxed completely as only trained muscles can. But their eyes were never still, roaming the vast and almost trackless wilderness which was more home to them than any house, lingering over each well-remembered ridge and peak and canyon. Presently

John stirred. Watching out of the corner of his eye, the ranger saw him pull a much-thumbed envelope out of his jacket and read the letter it contained.

John frowned over the letter and then, without a word, handed it to Crawford. The ranger read:

*Dear John:*

*I suppose by now you've practically forgotten who I am. But I surely haven't forgotten you or the swell times we had last summer.*

*This will probably give you a laugh, but I liked it so well out there that I got the idea I'd be a forester myself. So when I entered college last fall I went into the Forestry School.*

*What I've got on my mind now is this. Would there be any chance of getting a job working for you and Mr. Crawford this summer? I remember you told me that everyone starts in the same place in the Forest Service, in a lookout tower, but I don't know how to go about applying. So, if it isn't too much trouble, would you show me the ropes? That ought to feel natural since you spent most of last summer doing it.*

*Please give my best to Mr. Crawford, and my father sends his best to both of you. He says you don't really need to hire me because we'll both be out there anyway, and look at all the work you got out of us last year. But you know the way he talks. I'm serious.*

*Surely hope you can give me the information about applying, and that I'll be seeing you.*

*As ever,*

*Hank Winton*

Crawford handed the letter back with a chuckle and the comment: "A great pair, those Wintons. Will you ever forget that Senator peeling spuds?" But his eyes were watchful.

Stemple looked at him for a moment with a puzzled expression, as if expecting him to say something more. At last he blurted, "But what about all this, Hank studying forestry and wanting to go on a lookout tower? What d'you think?"

"I think it's the best news I've heard this spring. I suppose you wrote him to be out here for guard school and notified the Forest that we have a candidate."

"I haven't answered him at all," admitted John miserably. "I don't know what to do."

There was a little pause. Then Crawford said, "I must be a little slow on the uptake today. Because I don't get it." But he was careful not to look at John, for his eyes betrayed the fact that he understood perfectly and was merely waiting for his friend to confide in him.

It came with a rush. John said, "But don't you see, boss? Hank's just glamor-struck. What he got last summer was the movie version of forestry—fearless rangers battling the red enemy—headline stuff. He doesn't know the grind of it, year after year—cutting trail, splicing telephone lines, making out reports; working your heart out in summer, starving all winter because the politicians won't put up enough money to keep a crew all year. And then, about the time you're ready for your permanent appointment, some dude firefighter drops a snag on you.

"I couldn't stand that for Hank, boss. I owe him too much, him and his father. They saved my job and my life last summer. And that little deal in the snow-slide sort of convinced me. Suppose Hank couldn't take it. He has no idea of the cold-blooded way we pour it onto a first-year lookout. We try to break him, because we have to, and a lot of them we do break.

Or suppose his protection failed and he got burned up in a hot storm. What would we say to his father then?"

The shrewd, kindly eyes of the ranger met John's worried gaze at last. "You are mixed up, aren't you?" he remarked. "It will take me the rest of the way from here to the ranger station to straighten you out. But before we start, I'll just give you a general idea. Everything you've said is true, but you're all wrong."

Even John had to smile at that. They helped each other into their packs and faced upriver where the level rays of the afternoon sun were gilding each tree and filling the air with a golden haze.

"Now," said Crawford. As he talked his voice took on the plunging rhythm of his stride. "A guy writes to us and says he's in Forestry School and wants a lookout job for the summer. That's the way they all start, isn't it? You, me, the Supervisor and on up. But you say the guy is only glamor-struck. What a crust on your part!"

"Now wait a minute," protested John. "I didn't mean——"

"Quiet!" bellowed the ranger. "You had your say. Passing over a lot of tripe about working your heart out in summer and starving in winter—odd, what a

healthy bunch these overworked and underfed foresters are! You supposed a lot of terrible things that
might happen. Well, let's just suppose that our friend
Hank turned out to be a sockdolager of a forester,
which is my opinion. Of course, I like the inquisitive,
overgrown cuss, and think his father would want him
to have his chance, while you claim he couldn't take
it."

Again Stemple made frantic protest and again he
was shouted down. Thus the argument raged and
made the long miles short. Later, after dark, the two
foresters stretched their tired legs to the fire in the
Three Rivers Ranger Station. They had eaten well
and their wet clothes steamed on the drying wire behind the stovepipe.

Crawford twisted the dials of the big radio-tele-
phone. He had established contact with Forest Service headquarters in Midvale, a mountain range and
many canyons distant.

The speaker chuckled. "Midvale back to Three
Rivers. You just had to get in there, didn't you, you
old mountain goat?" The ghostly voice was recognizable as that of the Regional Forester himself, who
had a way of being near the radio when his men took
the field. "Have you anything else for us? Go ahead."

"Three Rivers to Midvale. One more thing. I'd like the following telegram sent. To Mr. Hank Winton, Eastern University, New Oxford, Pennsylvania: 'Report for smokechaser school June 10, Boundary Ranger Station, near Midvale, Montana.' Sign my name and turn Winton's registration over to the school director. Three Rivers clear with Midvale and standing by."

"Roger on your last message, Three Rivers. Good luck. Midvale off the air."

In his corner, Stemple sat complacently listening and the worry wrinkles in his forehead had vanished.

# T W O

Smokechaser School

HANK WINTON stood at the intersection of a
macadam highway and a narrow dirt road where the
bus from Midvale had let him off. He faced a sign-
board which read:

> **Boundary Ranger Station**
> **EVERGREEN NATIONAL FOREST**
> ½ mile

An arrow pointed down the dirt road and Hank could
see the station. It was at the edge of a broad, green
meadow, half surrounded by lodgepole pines which
marched in military fashion down a low hill. The
station was unmistakable in its orderly array of log
buildings, corrals and pastures. But it bore a further
sign: the flag of the United States rippling in a light
breeze. As every forester knows, that means a Forest

17

Service headquarters with its principal officer on duty.

Hank appeared to be in no hurry. He stood there, a big-boned, tow-headed six footer. At rest he looked a little awkward, for big as he was he had not yet quite filled out to the size of his hands and feet. But when he moved it was with the assurance and power of a lad who had won his numerals on a championship freshman football team.

He wore the uniform of the wilderness. And at an eastern university, it had cost him much trouble and some embarrassment to collect. But his denim jeans were properly faded and stagged off with a pocket knife halfway to the knee. His plaid shirt, also faded, was still a battle cry in color and his leather jacket was well scuffed. He lacked the battered and sweat-stained felt hat, but his thatch of straw-colored hair was unruly enough to make up for it. The only incongruous note was his footgear, a pair of well-polished oxfords. But he had the remedy in his packsack, a pair of the finest handmade steel-caulked logger's boots that money could buy. He had not quite dared to wear them on the train. The thought of those needle-pointed caulks against soft plush had made even him shudder.

Inside, Hank was a strange jumble of emotions. At the ranger station he would begin his apprenticeship as a forester in the smokechaser school. And in the mountains whose forest-mantled slopes loomed beyond the station, his body, brain and nerves would be put to the test. It was a dream come true. But his joy was tinged with uneasiness. As he stood beside the road, on the threshold of a career, the Forest Service looked very big and indifferent and he felt very small and unimportant.

He had allowed himself to believe that Stemple might meet him at the train. He had counted on having John's knowledge and prestige at his elbow during those moments when he must march up to a strange forester and say, "I'm Hank Winton, first-year man." But John had not come, had not even sent a message, and he must face it alone.

"What am I jittering about?" he chided himself. "They don't eat lookouts." He picked up his pack, slung it over one shoulder, and walked boldly up the middle of the road toward the ranger station. But he felt as if he were walking toward Fate.

As he came to the buildings, he was aware of the normal sights and sounds that go with a forest headquarters. From a shop to one side came the tormented shriek of a saw being filed. In the blacksmith shop near the round catching corral and the hitch racks, someone was shaping a horseshoe with the two light taps and then the full ringing whang. Out an open window of the headquarters building drifted the characteristic chant of a radio operator trying to push an electronic voice to some faraway ear. Several men crossed the yard on errands of their own, paying Hank not the slightest attention—to his relief.

He hesitated in front of the headquarters, reading the signs: "District Ranger's Office," "Fire Dispatcher," "Emergency Tool Cache." And then his eyes saw the placard tacked below one of the signs: "Guard School—Register Here." Hank dropped his pack near the door and went in.

Immediately he was in the atmosphere of the Forest Service, from the caulk-scarred floor to the map-covered walls and the smell of leather and oily metal. A brisk man in Forest green looked up at him from a pile of charts he was sorting and gave him a cheerful, "Hello. What can we do for you?"

Hank's throat was frozen, but he managed to squeeze out, "Name's Winton. I was told to report here for smokechaser school."

"Oh yes, Winton. You're one of Crawford's men."

The way he said "one of Crawford's men" made it something special. With the speed of conjury, several forms were whipped onto the desk and a pen appeared in Hank's fist while the man went on talking. "Sign here, and here and here. Get a sleeping bag out of the warehouse. The bunkhouse is over across the yard. You'll find all the other candidates there. You're the last one in. They'll show you the way to the cook shack and so on. Supper at five-thirty. First meeting of the school at six in the room upstairs here. Here's a message for you."

The last words fairly blew Hank out the door and before he really knew what was happening, he was outside with his pack in one hand and a slip of paper in the other. Dazedly he read the note.

It said: "Crawford and I are in Three Rivers, getting the district ready. We'll both be in at the end of the school when the lookouts are assigned. Good luck, boy. The school is tough. John."

The bunkhouse was such a bedlam as only twenty eighteen-year-olds can create within four walls. Old acquaintances yelled greetings across the room, beds were being dragged back and forth, nails driven and bags unpacked. No one took any direct notice of Hank, yet they managed to absorb him. One lad gave him a grin; another called, "One more victim." A slim six-footer said, "If you're looking for a bunk, there's an empty there in the corner."

Hank thanked him and dropped his pack and sleeping bag. At that moment a bell clanged. Amid cries of "Eats. Come and get it before he throws it out; women and children last," the smokechasers stampeded out the door, carrying Hank with them. He was not to learn for days that he had just spoken to Brad Davis, famous skier, victor over a renegade trapper in a winter race the length of Three Rivers.

Half an hour later, after the kind of meal that only logging-camp and Forest Service cooks can prepare, the same group assembled in the big upstairs room of the headquarters. Their high spirits were in check now. They sat on long benches, trying to look unconcerned, actually throbbing with eagerness and curiosity. Facing them was a small group of older men in Forest green, gathered around a plain board table, men with the stamp of authority and experience.

Hank heard whispers around him: "That's the Regional Forester . . . Aw, peddle that somewhere else . . . It is too, I tell you . . . Who's the big guy with the banged-up face? . . . Who is he? Don't you know anything? That's——"

The meeting started with no formality whatever. One of the foresters simply moved forward and spoke. "My name is Manley. I'm your Regional Forester. What I have to say won't take long. Each one of you wants to be a lookout-fireman and eventually a forester. I remind you that the job of lookout is exacting and very important. You boys on the towers are the nervous system of our fire-fighting organization, our eyes and our ears. Some of you are second-year men and you know what I mean when I say you will be severely tested. Good luck to you.

"For the practical details of the school, I turn you over to the Regional Fire Chief, Mr. Morrow. I'll be seeing you in the field."

The "big guy with the banged-up face" stepped forward. Fire Chief Morrow bore the scars of the terrible fire year of 1929 in which he had played a hero's role. He had eyes like tool steel under hairless brows and the grin of a sharpened axe.

He said, "I have a little bad news for you. There are twenty of you and only fifteen positions open. We didn't plan it that way but we don't mind. 'Competition is the spice of life,' or some such quotation. You are already a selected group. By every possible means we try to eliminate the glamor-struck, the casual and the merely curious. We have reason to believe that each one of you means business and I honestly wish we had places for you. But we don't, and, to be cold-blooded about it, you might as well learn now that this process of selection and elimination will go on from your first day in the Forest Service to your last."

Moving in the same abrupt way as he talked, the Fire Chief turned to the table behind him and picked up a heap of booklets. He handed them out to his tense audience, and then continued. "What you have there is the Fire Control Handbook, better known as the 'Smokechaser's Bible.' Each of you will keep it as long as he is a member of the forest fire organization. It contains everything we know about fighting fire from a one-man smoke to a thousand-man conflagration. I recommend it to you.

"The school will last three days. Your teachers are men with pine needles in their hair and their aim will be to give you a little practical experience with the tools and instruments of your trade. I guarantee you'll have a busy time.

"One more thing and I'm done. During the school period you will be introduced to a number of forms. You'll call it red tape and ask each other where the form is for when you scratch a mosquito bite. Admitting how irksome they are, I still tell you that they are necessary. They will all be read—your diaries, your work reports and your fire action records—read, studied and compared. Because we're always trying to learn, and the only way we can learn is from facts; what happened, where, when, and how and who did what about it.

"Now, good luck and I'll be seeing you on the fire line."

Soberly the lookouts filed down the stairway and into the yard. The afterglow was still in the western sky, the long June twilight hardly begun. But it seemed to Hank that a great change had come over his companions, so boisterous and carefree a few minutes earlier. Voices were subdued as they walked back toward the bunkhouse and each young would-be forester looked questioningly at his neighbor as if to ask, "Are you the one I have to beat?" Twenty candidates and only fifteen jobs. It was something to think about.

Hank thought and was not happy. He realized that he had come here thinking of himself as someone special, "one of Crawford's men." Now, all of a sudden, he was Hank Winton, no more and no less, on his own for the first time in his life. It was frightening to have all the familiar props knocked out from under him at once. How could he hope to compete with these others? Most of them had been raised in the West. Half of them were second-year men. You could actually pick them out because they weren't worried. They'd been through the mill. They had a tendency to herd by themselves in one end of the bunkhouse and their talk was full of Forest Service slang—rag camps, hot points, getaway time, azimuths, alidades, backsights, foresights, Class C fires and so on until Hank wondered if they were using a foreign language.

He sat down on the edge of his bed and tried to tell himself that a fellow could learn it all if he wanted to enough and wasn't a complete dope. Hank wished for Stemple or his father, someone to talk it over with. Amid twenty boys his own age, he was lonely, lonelier than at any other time he could remember. And that was odd in itself, because ordinarily he would have been calling half his companions by their first names in an hour.

Something pulled his gaze up from the floor to meet a pair of black eyes looking steadily at him from the next bed. Hank turned away quickly, embarrassed, but not before getting a mental picture of his neighbor. As completely at ease and relaxed as a cat, the other lookout was stretched on his back. His hair was as black as his eyes and he had the broadest shoulders Hank had ever seen. Without moving a muscle or saying a word, he gave an impression of self-confidence and controlled energy.

As if talking to the ceiling, he said, "Don't let those brass hats get your goat. It's the same fight talk they give every year."

Hank's heart gave a leap. Someone to talk to, and a second-year man at that, obviously a friend! He said, "They really lay it on the line, though, don't they?"

"And they'll give you a fair chance to show your stuff," replied the stranger. "What more do you want?"

"Nothing," admitted Hank. "My name's Hank Winton. What's yours?"

This casual gesture of friendliness had an unexpected result. The black-haired smokechaser sat halfway up and then dropped back. His eyes snapped round to Hank's face and away again. "Jim Dade's the name," he said. "It wouldn't mean anything to you."

He might just as well have gone into another room and slammed the door. Hank took the blame on himself. Who was he to get familiar with a second-year man? Ruefully he told himself, "Don't be so doggoned smart, next time."

Looking round, he saw that one by one the lookouts were crawling into their sleeping bags. The night chill of the mountains was creeping into the room. Hank followed the example of the others. That was one thing at least he wouldn't have to learn in smokechaser school: how wonderful it feels to crawl cold into a sleeping bag and wait for the delicious warmth to steal over you.

"Fire in the hills! Roll out!"

This challenge, bellowed in through the bunkhouse door, had the same effect as pushing down the handle of a blasting machine. Twenty sleeping bags erupted. The lookouts shivered into their clothes, splashed cold water on themselves and each other at the wash rack, and raced for the dining hall. There they stuffed themselves with cereal and fried eggs, bacon, flapjacks and coffee.

"Eat up, boys," urged the cook. "There'll be days like this; then they'll get tougher."

In the big room above the offices, a lean, tanned forester was waiting for them, flanked by four others. Their Forest-green uniforms were shiny and faded with wear and their caulked boots were dusty. The head instructor began to speak before the last of the boys found his place on a bench.

"Minutes count—let's go," he quoted the firefighter's war cry with a grin. "You see before you the faculty of our little college. I do most of the talking. Five of you will be assigned to each of these other gentlemen. They'll answer the questions, see that you don't get lost or hurt, find you or tie you up if you do, and make little black marks in their little black books.

"This institution has no regular hours. We have a lot of ground to cover, mentally and physically, in three days. We'll just go until we drop and then get up and go again."

The chief instructor had a way of punctuating each sentence with his little smile. It made him seem enthusiastic and pleased with what he was doing. "We'll talk a few minutes about maps," he continued. "A map is one of the most beautiful inventions of man, if you understand it, and just a mess of wiggly lines if you don't. A map is like taking the top layer off a piece of country and shrinking it down to pocket size so you can carry it around with you. As long as you have a map and know how to read it, you can never be lost. You might not know where you are, where you came from or where you're going. But you can't be lost, because with your map you can find out.

"That's one of the two most important things about a map. The other is that if you have a map and some other guy has a copy of the same, you can tell him where he is, where he's been and where he's going. Even if you're miles apart and in opposite directions.

"You think that isn't so wonderful?" The instructor paused and seemed to share his grin with each lookout individually. "You're saying to yourselves, 'So I'm talking to Joe over on the other side of town and I tell him to meet me at the corner of Fourth and Main. What's wonderful about that?' But you and Joe are going to be on opposite sides of a mountain range. And a fire's going to start. You can see it. Joe can't, but he's closer to it than you are. And you're going to want to tell him to hump himself over there and put it out. Now where's the corner of Fourth and Main? It's at a big old lightning-struck fir in the middle of a million others just like it and none of them wearing any sign boards.

"How are you going to tell him now? Write him a twenty-page letter about the streams he has to cross and the mountains he has to climb and the cliffs he'd better dodge? Not if you want to get that fire out. No, you're going to look at your map. You see that it's divided up into squares and you know that each square is a mile along each side—what we call a section—and that it has a number: And each one of those squares can be divided into four smaller ones, called quarter-sections, and so on down. So all you say to Joe is this: 'Joe, my boy, there's a fine black smoke coming out of the northeast quarter of the southwest quarter of section twenty. Get a move on because she's hot.'

"And Joe, way off there in the tules, knows everything he needs to. Because he's got a map too. Now let's all go out in the woods and play Joe."

At the end of that first day Hank was convinced that nowhere else in the world could there be anything like the smokechaser school. He had worked hard in prep school, and all during his freshman year in college it had seemed that he could never quite catch up. But the smokechaser school was like a newsreel and moved with the same nightmarish speed from one exciting scene to another.

All in one day Hank had learned to use a map, really to use it. Then he had discovered the compass which, besides pointing north, performs all sorts of other little tricks in the hands of a forester. He had practised with the firefinder which is only a special sort of compass. And finally he had put all three together—map, compass and firefinder—and at last understood how a lookout perched on top of a mountain can pick out a column of smoke in the middle of a million-acre wilderness and send unerringly to it one man or a hundred from as many different directions.

There was very little activity in the bunkhouse after supper that night. The lookouts were tired physically and mentally. They crawled into their sleeping bags early. And though no one mentioned it, all were aware that even this soon, two bunks were empty. How or when two of their number had been found lacking and removed, no one knew. But they were gone. In the dark, each young lookout pondered that fact and went over and over his own day wondering if he was next. This one had misread his compass; that one had failed to note an impassable swamp across the map route he had picked to an imaginary fire. Hank squirmed each time he thought of a question he had asked, a dumb question, and how hard the group instructor had set him down for it.

It was midnight when that clarion voice rang through the room again: "Fire in the hills! Roll out!"

Befuddled with sleep, grumbling, the lookouts hustled into their clothes. In the chilly moonlight, they found the chief instructor. To each boy as he came up he handed a map, a compass, a Forest Service headlamp and a slip of paper.

When they were all gathered around him, he said, "The lookout on Tabletop has reported a number of fires. They are actual fires, started by your group instructors, though I'm afraid they're rather small and well hidden. Each of you has a Form 17, a Lookout Fire Report, showing the azimuth and distance of a fire from the lookout tower. Each of you will go to the fire indicated on his Form 17. At the fire you will complete Form 592, the Fireman's Report, and turn it over to your group instructor who will be at the fire. Then you can come home and sleep some more—if there's time. Tabletop has left his light burning so you can line up your compasses on him. I strongly advise you to travel independently. The guy you follow might have his readings balled up, or he might be going to a different fire. Good luck."

With that the chief instructor departed and left them looking alternately from their maps to that distant, low-lying star, the light in Tabletop.

"Then we'll get up and go some more," snorted an

unidentifiable voice. "And what beats me is no one told me I had to. I asked for this."

By the afternoon of the third day, the young smoke-chasers were a haggard, weary crew. Their minds were stuffed with a bewildering array of information about forest fires, their muscles ached from putting that information into actual practise. They had learned how to repair telephones and telephone lines, they had calculated fire danger on the Fire Danger Meter. They had inspected and used firefighting tools and machines from pulaski and shovel on up through back pumps, motorized pumps, Bosworth trenchers and caterpillar tractors. Nervous tension was so high among them that they had almost stopped talking to one another. For there were still three of them to be eliminated. But their shoulders were square and their eyes were bright as they faced the last act in what had become, for them, not a school but a sort of blood-and-thunder melodrama.

The chief instructor explained: "Just to wind things up with a bang, we're going through the whole process of controlling a fair-sized fire. As usual, you will take all the parts. Some will be sent out as smoke-chasers, individually. The others will come along as reinforcements. What we're after is to give you a

Instructors as well as students had been on the fire line

chance to see fire-dispatching technique. What we want to leave with you is the knowledge that you're never alone. You may be all by yourself out there in the jungle with some fire getting ready to run over you. But you aren't alone. Somebody's on the way to help you and somebody else is moving up behind him —armies of men, truck- and plane-loads of supplies and equipment; pack-trains on every trail, eyes on every mountain, the air full of voices. All to back up you boys in the first line. Remember this if you don't remember anything else. You're never alone.

"Now report to your group instructors for your assignments. It's going to be a real thing."

At dusk, trucks brought the smokechasers back to the ranger station. They were dusty, red-eyed and trembling with fatigue. Sweat had smeared the soot on their faces and more than one had the naked look that goes with eyebrows singed off. The chief instructor had not lied to them. It had been a real fire. In fact it had been so real that for a while instructors as well as students had been on the fire line. Now, wondering what could possibly happen next and too tired to care, they were herded into the big room in headquarters.

Then, before a word could be spoken, they came to

life. The room was already part full of men, steel shod, in faded uniforms and battered felt hats, men "with pine needles in their hair." The rangers and their alternates had come in from all the far-flung districts of the Forest. They were gathered round a table to which were tacked eighteen small white cards.

Tonight the lookouts would be chosen.

The bold crowded forward to stare; the uncertain hung back. Hank, taller than most of the others, could look over the crowd. Immediately he picked out the commanding head of Crawford and the trim, active figure of Stemple. They saw him too. Crawford nodded and Stemple raised a hand. Hank felt his heart come up into his throat. He wanted to get down on his hands and knees and crawl out of the room. Surely, if he were among the chosen, they would have given him a sign.

Naturally he could not know that the rangers had been drifting in all the afternoon. Out there choked with smoke and heat, he could hear no hint of the wrangle which had been going on right up to the moment when the student lookouts returned.

"What kind of a hocus-pocus is this?" one ranger had snarled to Crawford. "You've already got Jim Dade and Brad Davis and Hjalmar Sorensen, the best of the second-year men and oldtimers. Now you walk right up and grab this Winton kid, the best of the new crowd."

"Now Tom," Crawford had soothed. "Just because you got in late and missed getting first pick for once, don't blow your gaskets. You know you haven't got a man you'd trade me."

They weren't really angry. But it would have been news to the smokechasers to know that the competition among the rangers for the most promising new men was as savage as it had been among themselves.

All Hank knew was that a voice began droning: "Assigned to Three Rivers District: James Dade, Bradley Davis, Henry Winton."

The room was spinning round him and as it began to empty a familiar hand grasped his and a familiar voice said, "Welcome to Three Rivers, smokechaser."

# THREE

## *Reunion*

IT SEEMED to Hank Winton that he was a different person. In a number of invisible but important ways, he actually was. He knew things he hadn't known before; that a "rag camp," for instance, is a temporary lookout point set up in a tent and only manned during times of extreme fire danger. He could read a compass, backsight, foresight, azimuth and declination; he could look at a map and tell you what kind of country it represented: how steep the ridges, how thick the timber growing on them, and which way the streams ran. He fancied that he could swing a pulaski with the next man. He was a smoke-chaser, duly appointed and assigned. All this he had gained by his own effort, with his own brain and muscles. And that is a milestone in anyone's life.

Many things he still had to learn. Ahead of him lay tests beyond anything he had met in smokechaser school. But he was mercifully unaware of them. With his packsack slung on one shoulder and his sleeping bag balanced on the other, he left the already half-deserted bunkhouse. He took the bag to the warehouse and tossed it through the door with a casual, "Thanks for the use of your bye-bye bundle," to the man on duty.

Then he swaggered across the yard, grinding his caulks jubilantly into the unoffending earth, toward a dusty Forest-green pickup. He was a forester going to hold reunion with his kind, with Crawford and John Stemple.

During the short trip to Midvale, Stemple and Hank plied each other with questions. How was everything in Three Rivers? When was Senator Winton coming out? Whatever became of so-and-so and so-and-so? They acted as if they hadn't seen each other for years instead of a few months.

As they turned off the main highway and began to thread the tree-shaded streets of the residential district, John explained, "We're having supper and spending the night at the boss's house. Tomorrow we'll fly in to the District. That will sure beat pounding seventy-five miles of trail."

Hank did not answer for so long a time that Stemple looked at him inquiringly and asked, "What's on your mind?"

Hank came out of his reverie with a start and said, "It's hard to put it into words. But whenever I think of Crawford it's how I saw him last summer during the fire, with maps, radios and telephones all around him; a dozen people waiting for him to tell them what to do; holding the whole works together twenty-four hours a day and all the time so calm and easy about it while the rest of us were going crazy. I just can't picture him with a home and a family."

"I know what you mean," replied John. "But you might as well get used to the idea. He's a human being too, when he gets the chance, and has a darn nice family."

He parked the truck before a house that might just as well have been any other in the block. They were all well-built and comfortable looking with flower beds and deep lawns. Almost reluctantly Hank followed his companion up the walk. He wasn't sure that he *wanted* to see Crawford as a man with a home and a family.

John, as one familiar with the place, opened the door without knocking and went in, Hank on his heels. They entered a living room panelled in knotty pine, where a fire blazed on an open hearth and a silken-haired setter thumped his tail in lazy welcome. Whatever it was Hank had expected, it was not this. Men sat in the leather armchairs and the room was full of the fragrance of pipe smoke and their deep laughter.

By themselves on a couch yet still part of the group sat a tall woman and a slender girl who was obviously her daughter. The men merely looked up and waved careless hands in greeting, but Mrs. Crawford and her daughter got up and came toward the newcomers. Hank thought they were the handsomest pair he had ever seen.

"Oh, oh," he whispered to John. "Now I know what you meant about a darn nice family." And a glance at Stemple's fiery ear told him he had hit the target.

Then before he could think up any more teasing remarks he was swept into a round of introductions. John introduced him to Mrs. Crawford and Dorothy Crawford. Then, in quick succession, he got a word of welcome from the ranger and met Lane and Bob Corbett. Brad Davis, the last member of the party, said, "Hank and I have already met, at the school.

Sure glad you're going to be on the District with us."

Then Mrs. Crawford and Dorothy disappeared with a word about supper. John went with them and the others picked up the thread of their conversation. The ranger and the two Corbetts were in the middle of some forestry argument far over Hank's head, though Brad Davis was listening attentively. It was a relief to Hank that they appeared to have forgotten him. Quietly he moved to the farthest corner of the room, conscious for the first time in days of the size of his hands and feet. He had never felt so out-of-place and unnecessary in his life. It it hadn't been for John, he would have tried to sneak out of the house.

Presently Dorothy Crawford reappeared, looked the room over once and then came unerringly to his corner. "What in the world are you doing here off by yourself?" she asked in a low voice.

Hank looked at her and saw that it was an honest question. There was no mockery in her gray eyes. Besides, she was John Stemple's girl and the urge to confide in someone was overpowering.

"I don't belong here," he said miserably. "Lane and Bob Corbett, Brad Davis, your father—why, they're the tops, they're famous. You read about the things they've done in newspapers all over the country. And I'm a punk, just out of smokechaser school. I ought to be under this house, not in it."

The girl heard him out in complete seriousness. "That's right," she said. "You're only Hank Winton, the guy who dragged Johnny Stemple out of the middle of the Moose Lake fire last year and the only one who had sense enough to give him artificial respiration when he was dying of smoke pneumonia." Suddenly she grinned at him, looking amazingly like her father as she did it. "I think you can eat in the same room with us, Hank. Come on and help us set the table."

Hank Winton felt himself expanding to his normal size as he followed her out of the room. But deep inside him there was a small ache. It was the pain of knowledge, of understanding at last something he had learned in the savage competition of smokechaser school. He understood now that he could be at ease in Crawford's house, but this was not the reunion he had dreamed of with John and the ranger. That reunion could never be until he had proved himself as a forester.

But at least he no longer wanted to crawl off in a corner and hide. Dorothy Crawford, with a few straight words, had done that for him. Until events proved otherwise, he was entitled to hold his head erect and meet even the Corbett brothers on equal terms.

Mrs. Crawford gave him a quick smile as he came into the kitchen. Dorothy pointed to a stack of plates and nodded toward the dining room. Brad, quietly chewing something he had filched out of the refrigerator, exchanged solemn winks with him.

As they were setting out the plates, Dorothy said, "I'm going to spend part of the summer at Three Rivers. If it isn't too far, I'll ride up and see you. What tower will you be on?"

"Nobody's told me yet," replied Hank. "But the way I understand it, the greenhorns always draw the hottest points. So it will probably be Sliderock, Gray Plume, or Copper Mountain."

The girl looked at him understandingly. "And you can hardly wait," she said. "I envy you . . . but I hope it isn't Sliderock."

# FOUR

~~~~~~~~~~~~~~~~~~~~~~~~

## *Jim Dade*

TWO days went by as rapidly as if Hank had dreamed them. There was the flight from Midvale to Three Rivers, certainly an adventure into unreality. It was the second trip of the day, Hank learned. Brad Davis and Jim Dade had gone in on the early flight. But he recognized Ben Gray, the dispatcher, among the trail foremen, radio and telephone technicians, packers and other smokechasers who crowded the cabin.

The plane took off from a crowded port, from among sleek airliners. Loudspeakers quarreled with the horns of taxicabs, the boundary fences were crowded with people in bright summer clothes. And in a matter of minutes the flight ended on a meadow where the only sound was the soft thunder of a wilderness river; the only onlookers, a band of deer who raised their white flags and bounced away among the trees.

Hank had shared a bale of cargo parachutes with a little old gnome of a man with a face so weathered and wrinkled it was like gingerbread with two bits of ice for eyes. He introduced himself as Hjalmar Sorensen in the voice of a deep-toned bell—with a Norwegian accent.

Hank's amazement was complete when he discovered that Sorensen was a lookout and had spent ten seasons in Three Rivers. It was his second contact with a strange and slowly disappearing race of men. Hjalmar Sorensen was one of the "oldtimers," men who joined the Forest Service when it was new and had worked for it all their lives without thought of advancement, simply because they loved the wilderness. Ageless, uneducated, but woodsmen beyond compare, they had seen the Service grow great and strong under the guidance of the fledgling foresters they had trained. And more than one had laid down his life for the Forest, like Paddy Brennan, John Stemple's foster-father, whom Hank had known before he died in the great Moose Lake fire.

Hank would gladly have listened to Hjalmar all day for the music of his voice alone. But half an hour after the plane landed, Stemple called him into the office. With a start, Hank realized that already most

of the men who had flown in with him had disappeared into the wilderness. Crawford looked up at
him from a map-strewn desk. He was no longer a
man with a family and a home, but a commander in
the field.

He gave Hank orders crisply. "You're to start upriver immediately. You'll spend tonight at Indian
Battleground. You'll find a crew there, rebuilding
the station. Tomorrow you move on up to the Puzzle
Basin smokechaser cabin. You'll be there for the next
few weeks until the fire season starts. Instructions for
maintenance and repair work are already at the cabin.
When the fire season starts, you'll be stationed on
Sliderock."

John was standing so close to Hank that their
shoulders touched, and at the word "Sliderock" Hank
felt the alternate ranger's start. But he said nothing
and Crawford did not seem to notice.

The ranger concluded with one of his characteristic smiles, like the curved flash of an axe-blade.
"We'll be seeing you, John and I, when we can get
up your way. Good luck, and always believe your
compass."

And now Hank was, according to his map, within
a mile of his destination. He had followed the main-

line trail along the river to Indian Battleground where he had spent the night. From the "log mechanics" who were rebuilding it, he had heard again the story of how a renegade trapper had burned the station the winter before as a means of escaping from Brad Davis and his uncles, the Corbett brothers.

At the junction of the Wolf and Sable Rivers, he had crossed the latter on a footbridge and continued on a dimmer trail up the dwindling Wolf. His caulks made no sound on the carpet of pine needles. All around him was the vast hush of the climax forest, a hush peopled with the small sounds of the woods folk. Now and again, through a break in the massed tree trunks, he caught a glimpse of towering ridges. Down the canyons that ran between came singing mountain streams. And once, from a little meadow, he saw a lone peak, a shaft of living rock rising out of a colossal heap of fragments, still sheathed in ice, and on its very pinnacle a spidery tower of glass. He looked at his map and checked direction with his compass. Then he was sure, and with heart beating more quickly, he looked up at Sliderock.

Having allowed him that one glimpse, the incredible mountain veiled itself in clouds. In one of those dramatic changes only possible in the high country, the sky turned black instantaneously. All the giant evergreens sighed and the aspens shook their new leaves madly. Rain slashed down among the trees, turned to a brief patter of hail and then snow, great soggy flakes that made Hank feel as though he were being slapped in the face with a wet brush.

It was a spring blizzard much like the one which had caught Stemple and Crawford a short time earlier. It soaked Hank and chilled him through in a moment. He could have taken shelter under a spruce whose lowspread and overlapping branches were proof even against a mountain storm. But it never occurred to him to do so. He almost welcomed the discomfort, because it was real and meant that he, Hank Winton, was really here.

Though they had rattled off nearly ten miles, his long legs bore him with a jaunty swing through the dripping woods. Every few moments his hand went to the flap of his shirt pocket to make sure that a certain bit of metal had not come unfastened. It was only a piece of brass, cut in the form of a tiny shield and with a pine tree stamped on its face. But it was also real and to his fingers it glowed, for it was the badge of a forester.

The storm, having had its fun and reminded the

world that spring in the high Rockies is no matter of mild showers and soft breezes, withdrew to the peaks as suddenly as it had come. As he tossed the wet mane of yellow hair out of his eyes, Hank saw the clouds open like gigantic doors on a sky so blue that it hurt to look at it. Sunlight poured through upon him and upon a weathered, rain-streaked cabin in the center of a tiny alpine park. Vapor began to rise from the cabin's roof, and on every blade of grass the water droplets burned like diamonds.

In this flood of light and warmth after the storm, with the smell of clean earth and growing things in his nostrils and bird songs in his ears, Hank approached his destination. This would be his home for the few weeks before the fire season began. Here he would harden his muscles and sharpen all the nerves and senses that grow dull in cities. He would learn the tricks of his trade: to swing an axe and file a saw, to repair a telephone, adjust a fire-finder; to be as familiar with this wilderness as his own backyard; to cook his own meals and darn his own socks. Most important of all, he would learn to depend upon himself, the first law of the woodsman.

Not that any such ideas went through his mind. A few yards from the cabin he paused and his thought was how snug and natural it looked. With the inquisitive, trusting brown eyes of a yearling colt, and half smiling, he read the sign over the cabin door:

> **Puzzle Basin Guard Station**
> **Three Rivers District**
> **EVERGREEN NATIONAL FOREST**

A thrill ran along his nerves as he realized suddenly why the name Puzzle Basin was familiar. It was from this cabin in midwinter that Brad Davis had started his hundred-mile chase on skis after Emil Sicard, the renegade who had burned Indian Battleground. To think that he was going to live in the same place, work with men like Davis and Crawford and Stemple, made him breathe faster. Then he shied like a nervous horse, for the cabin door had opened and he was face to face with a stranger.

For a moment the two studied each other. What Hank saw framed in the doorway was a lad perhaps a year older than his eighteen. He was black-haired and black-eyed, with high cheekbones and a way of holding his chin in against his chest. Estimating him in terms of football, Hank said to himself, "Wow!

What a running guard!" Almost a head shorter than Hank, he was tremendously broad in the shoulders and long in the arms. And he was not a stranger after all.

"Why I know you!" exclaimed Hank delightedly. "You're Jim Dade. I bunked beside you at guard school."

"I know you too," replied Dade. But in his voice there was no pleasure and no welcome. "They telephoned you were on your way up," he continued in the same flat, surly tone. "I wasn't expecting you so soon. Trust a dude to bull his way through a storm instead of riding it out under a spruce. Well, come on in and get dry."

Hank followed Dade into the cabin, amazed. It was the first time in his life that anyone had been deliberately unfriendly. He couldn't believe that Dade meant it. They had never seen each other before except during the hectic three days at guard school. And there Dade had ignored him after that one venture in the bunkhouse.

All this went through his mind in a flash. By the time he was inside the cabin Hank had decided that the trouble was in his imagination. He was tired himself and no doubt Dade had been working hard too

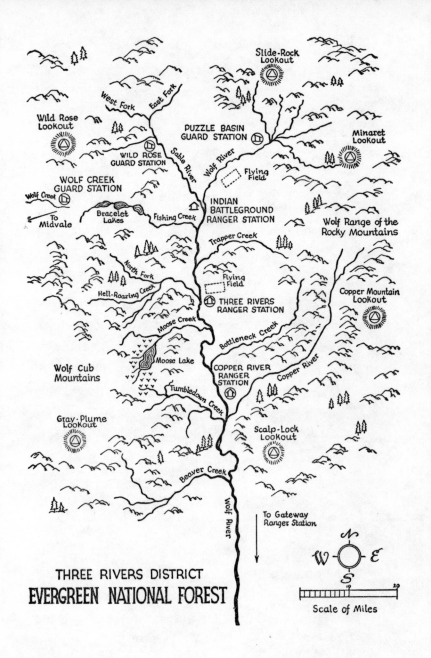

THREE RIVERS DISTRICT
EVERGREEN NATIONAL FOREST

Scale of Miles

that day. He grew enthusiastic all over again, for it was unexpected luck to be assigned to a station with Jim Dade, a second-year man. In other words, Dade had survived the ruthless weeding out of his own first year on a lookout tower and now his feet were planted firmly on the ladder up which every man goes, step by step, in the Forest Service. It would be an education to work with him for a few weeks before going out on his own.

Nevertheless, Hank decided to let Dade make the next move. He remembered how suddenly the lookout had drawn back into himself at smokechaser school. He remembered also what a time he and his father had gone through the summer before making friends with John Stemple. That was a little different, of course. They had been dudes then and Stemple a forester wrongly suspected of deserting a fire. But maybe Jim was the same stiff-necked, ingrowing type. The thing was to approach him gradually.

While he dug dry clothes out of his packsack, Hank's eyes were busy. He had never been inside a smokechaser cabin before and he was doubly curious about everything, because now this was *his* cabin—his and Dade's. He stole a glance at the other lookout and was rewarded with a view of a broad, square back leaning over the stove. But it was not broad enough to cut off a delicious smell of cooking food. He could feel his mouth begin to water.

The Puzzle Basin guard station was a one-room cabin built of peeled logs weathered to a soft brown and so beautifully fitted at the corners that one could hardly slip a knife blade into the joints. It had a high-pitched roof to withstand the weight of the deep snows of winter and a deep porch where firewood was stacked level with the windows.

It was small, so small that there was no place in it for anything that did not have a practical use. The stove where a coffee pot steamed and Dade bent over a savory-smelling kettle occupied one corner. Near it was a wall cabinet with a door that swung down to make a table. The cabinet itself, Hank noted, was loaded with everything imaginable to eat in cans, boxes and packages. If a man went hungry in the Forest Service it would certainly be his own fault. The back of the room was filled almost completely by a double-deck steel bunk. There was room in each corner for a person to store his extra belongings. Not much room, but foresters travel light.

Planks were laid across the rafters overhead and on these planks was stacked the forest-fire fighter's arsenal. There were shovels and picks, the long, thin steel ribbons of two-man saws, double-bitted axes, and pulaskis, those marvelous firefighting weapons half axe and half grub hoe named for the famous old-time ranger who invented them. The afternoon sun peering in at the windows glittered on all their honed and polished edges.

In a corner of their own hung several "man-killers," the firefighter's packs which contain everything a man needs for a two-day battle with the red enemy of the wilderness.

Finally, the cabin was spotlessly clean, windows gleaming, walls freshly painted and the floor, pitted by the caulks of many a forester, scrubbed bone white. And that was another law of the Forest Service.

Hank had changed his clothes and hung the wet ones on the drying wire behind the stove. He would have liked to offer to help Dade with supper, but there seemed to be nothing for him to do. The table was set, the wood box and water buckets were full. Most of all he would have liked to start a conversation. He was bursting with questions and it seemed inhuman to him for two people meeting in the heart of the wilderness not to compare notes. But there was something in the set of Dade's shoulders and the way all his attention was focussed on his cooking that kept Hank quiet.

At last Dade put the kettle and the coffee pot on the table and without looking at Hank said, "Well, soup's on. Aren't you going to report to HQ?"

Hank felt his neck begin to burn. It was a fine way to start off his career as a forester: by forgetting his duty to report his whereabouts every time he came to a telephone. Even last summer as a dude he had learned that much and how important it was for the people at headquarters to know the location of every man.

He went to the telephone and rang the Three Rivers Ranger Station, so embarrassed that when the voice of John Stemple answered he did not recognize it. He said, "Winton, reporting in at Puzzle Basin."

"Glad to have you with us, Winton," replied Stemple with equal formality. Then he chuckled. "How's it going, Hank? Did that storm catch you?"

"Sure did. All I needed was a bar of soap and I could have had washday." John's friendly voice brought the glow back in a rush.

"There'll come a day when you'll pray for a storm like that," laughed the alternate ranger. "See you in the morning." Foresters always "see" each other on the telephone or radio. Perhaps it is because they spend so much of their lives not seeing anyone at all.

When he turned from the telephone, Hank found that Dade had already started to eat. He sat down and helped himself, making a mental note that while his companion might be no talker, he was certainly a cook. The stew in the big kettle was seasoned just right. There was a big plate of baking-powder biscuits flanked by butter and jam, half a chocolate cake and, wonder of wonders, a golden-brown pie cut in quarters and filling the air with the rich scent of apples.

The two ate as only young fellows living outdoors and working hard can. It was so good that Hank forgot his resolution to let Dade make the next opening. "Man," he said, pushing back his plate, "that was really fine. Sure hope I can learn to cook like that."

In reply he got a flash of Dade's black eyes and six words: "Uncle furnishes everything including a cookbook."

There the conversation ended. But Hank was content as he filled a pan with hot water and went to work washing the dishes. He thought he detected, in Dade's gruff answer, a hint of unbending, like a dog who growls and wags his tail at the same time. If he had been a little older he would have realized that the good cook never lived who could resist a compliment on his skill.

At this same moment, all unknown to the two young smokechasers, both their natures were under older and wiser observation. At the Three Rivers Ranger Station, twenty-odd miles away, Crawford and Stemple were also relaxing after supper. They were in the ranger's quarters. Crawford, with his immensely tall and powerful body sprawled over a chair, one table and part of another, was a picture of informality few people were privileged to see. Stemple was kneeling on his own chair, leaning over the table and trying to read a map partially hidden by the ranger's legs.

Crawford blew a cloud of pipe smoke which only half hid the twinkle in his eye as he said, "I heard you talking to your protégé over the phone. How does he like it at Puzzle Basin?"

"O.K., he said," replied Stemple without looking up. "You know, our fuel map is way out of date on this area at the head of Beaver Creek. If that ever gets touched off it will blow higher than Mt. Mc-Kinley."

"Quit changing the subject," snorted the ranger. "All day you've been acting as if I'd chopped a rock with your pet axe. Now out with it. What's grinding on you?"

John straightened up and looked him in the eyes. "My protégé!" he blurted. "You sold me on the idea that Hank would take his chances along with the other new men. But I didn't figure that meant you'd sentence him to two or three weeks with Jim Dade—and assign him to Sliderock."

"But Hank's the best of the new lookouts. You saw the school records yourself," protested the ranger. "Why wouldn't I assign him to Sliderock? Dade was our star pupil last year and he made his mark on Sliderock, didn't he?"

"That's one way of looking at it. The other is that it's the hottest point on the Forest and we've had two lookouts burnt up on it."

The ranger dropped his bantering tone. His lean, weather-darkened face was serious as he answered, "The protection on that tower is solid; the lightning expert from the Regional office rebuilt it and I checked it. All of which you know. John, you've got this all wrong, because you think so much of that kid. You're afraid it's going to be too tough for him. Sure, we can put him on some dinky, low-level tower and ease him through. Nothing simpler. But what will happen when we aren't around to take care of him, when he goes out to some strange district? No, he thinks he wants to be a forester and now is the time to find out if he can take the grief that goes with it. We'll make him quick or bust him quick. In this game, it's the only way, and the most merciful."

There was a pause while John, never one for snap judgments, thought it over. At last he grinned and shrugged his shoulders, saying, "You're right, boss. You always are. But Dade—why couldn't we have put Hank out with someone human, like Brad Davis? That Dade will probably be a Regional Forester some day, but he gives me the creeps."

The ranger laughed. "I put them together on purpose. Dade makes it awfully hard to like him, but you know yourself there's no man on the District you'd rather have with you in a tight place. Hank likes everybody on sight. Maybe Hank will sweeten him up a little and get a little tougher himself."

"Just so that black-haired pug doesn't work Hank over," grumbled John. "If he does, he and I've still got a little unfinished business."

"Why, I didn't know you and Dade had ever mixed it," exclaimed Crawford with interest. "When was it and how did it come out?"

"One of the two things that happened on this District last year you didn't know all about," retorted John. "It came out a tie and I was lucky. That man is pure poison with his dukes."

"I don't think we'll have any trouble on those lines," said the ranger. "I warned Dade to leave his fighting clothes in Midvale or I'd run him clear out of the Forest Service, and as far as I can make him out, the Service is all he lives for. Hank will tame him and learn a lot in the process."

Far upriver, at Puzzle Basin, the taming was not going forward very rapidly. On opposite sides of the swinging table, under the glaring light of a gasoline pressure lamp, Jim Dade and Hank Winton were studying their smokechaser's bibles. Their entire evening's conversation had been:

Jim: "I'll make you a proposition, dude. I do all the cooking. You get the wood and water and do the cleaning up."

Hank (who could have prolonged such an offer into half an hour of joshing and horseplay): "It's a deal."

In the days that followed, Hank came to accept as a fact that Dade just wasn't a friendly type of person. After a few more rebuffs, he became as taciturn as

Dade himself, for Hank had the priceless gift of adaptability, of being able to get along in any situation. Fortunately he never dreamed that there was anything personal in the way Dade acted.

In spite of the fact that they exchanged scarcely a hundred words a day and those on business, he learned a great deal about his companion. He had to, for they were as isolated from the rest of the world as if they had been on an island. Twice a day, morning and evening, they reported to headquarters by telephone. The rest of the time they worked long hours at the endless task of maintaining the Forest. This meant principally going over the many miles of trail, those highways of the wilderness, and putting them into condition so that men and pack animals could move quickly. They cut out the winter's crop of fallen trees. They drained bog-holes and laid corduroy across swamps. They rebuilt bridges and footlogs over the turbulent mountain streams. For almost every mile of trail, there was a mile of telephone line which also needed looking after. It was hard work. It was interesting. Best of all, perhaps, it was satisfying, for at the end of a day a man could see what he had accomplished and know that it was well done.

It bothered Hank not to be able to break through

Jim's reserve, but not to the point where he lost any sleep over it. And there was this about it, Dade might deny him friendship but he could not deny Hank the right to learn from him. Dade had to teach him woodsmanship in sheer self-defense. They were working with edged tools and, often enough, under dangerous conditions. In its gargantuan, offhand way, the wilderness fought back at their efforts to bend it to their will.

Hank learned never to swing an axe without first looking over his shoulder for the springy tree limb that would deflect the blade into his own leg, or Jim's. He learned to make a tree fall in the right direction, but to stand clear in case it should playfully jump backward. He learned how to keep a saw from pinching and that if a lightning storm has been near, a telephone line may be carrying enough current to knock a man flat.

With every move he made, Jim showed himself to be an expert woodsman and Hank eagerly copied him. He even startled a grunt of commendation out of the dour young forester when it developed that Hank was ambidextrous, could chop or pull a saw as well left-handed as right. Occasionally, over a good meal, when they were both tired and relaxed, Dade unbent enough to talk a little if the subject was the Forest Service. Hank discovered that the way to get him started was to ask some particularly dumb question about the Fire Control Handbook, which they both studied constantly.

It was worth the inevitable sneer to listen while Dade explained the point in short, explosive sentences—and revealed a little of himself in the process. Surly and unfriendly the young woodsman might be, but he was Forest Service to the last drop of his blood, and with a driving ambition to climb high. So far, Hank had never had to fight or suffer enough for anything he wanted to understand such a fierce determination to excel. It puzzled and even frightened him a little. Also, to his own surprise, he realized that he was actually becoming fond of Jim and would do almost anything to earn his respect.

One day, after they had been together nearly two weeks, he thought he had found the way to Dade's heart. It was Saturday, when they stopped work at noon, and they were loafing. Several times Hank had noticed a set of boxing gloves under Jim's bed.

Now he spoke casually. "Say, I happened to notice those gloves under your bed. Are you a boxer, Dade?"

Watching out of the corner of his eye, he surprised

a strange look on Jim's face, a look compounded of eagerness and uncertainty and something else which Hank could not read but which gave him a momentary chill. It was plain that for once he had caught Jim's interest.

"Yeah, I've done a little boxing," replied Dade. "What of it? Want to go a round or two?"

"I wouldn't mind, just to work up a sweat," said Hank. "Don't know much about it, though."

Without further words, Dade went and got the gloves. The two put them on and, stripped to the waist, moved out to a level, grassy spot before the cabin. Dade scratched a rough circle in the turf with his caulks. "No timekeeper," he explained. "Whenever one of us steps outside the ring, that's a round."

Hank watched these businesslike preparations with a question in his mind, like a person who wakes up in a strange room and asks himself, "Now how did I get here?" He actually knew nothing whatever about boxing and had never before had on a pair of boxing gloves. They felt harsh and strange and awkward. It was equally plain that on Dade's hands they felt natural. Always sure and swift in all his movements, the black-haired young forester was now like a tiger, poised on the balls of his feet. His chin was tucked against his shoulder, his right glove close to it and his left half extended with little flicking motions.

"Isn't there anything this guy can't do better than I can?" thought Hank dolefully. He raised his own guard and pawed experimentally at his opponent. He could not see that Jim made any counter-move at all. But he felt something glide along his forearm, deflecting his clumsy blow. And then all at once his head exploded. Hank staggered back; his hands dropped while he tried to shake the stars out of his eyes.

"Short round, wasn't it?" sneered Dade.

Hank's vision cleared. Looking down, he saw that he had stepped out of the ring. Promptly he stepped in again. Good-natured and friendly as he was, Hank also had a temper, honestly inherited. In the halls of the United States Senate, the name Winton and fighter meant almost the same thing. And now Hank was angry as he had never been before in his life. He had expected a sparring match, with the object merely to touch your opponent with the gloves, not hurt him.

But Dade wanted to make a fight of it, and fighting, so Hank believed, was another matter. Confident in his superior height and weight, Hank waded in, slugging wildly. He could feel his gloves striking, he thought he was driving Dade back and that in a moment it would be his turn to say, "Short round, wasn't it?"

But there was something the matter with his eyes, for Dade was blurred before them and a series of light shocks kept running from his jaw all the way to his heels. Actually, he was merely flailing Dade's shoulders while Jim hammered him with a left that moved in and out with the precision and speed of a riveting gun.

The second round lasted a little longer, but ended in the same way as the first, with Hank outside the ring, shaking his dizzy head.

There was a salty taste in his mouth, his heart was thumping and his arms felt heavy as lead. He could not seem to get enough air into his lungs, and he knew now that he was beaten.

Before his addled mind dangled two facts. He knew that as often as he stepped inside the ring, Dade would pound him back again. And he knew that if he stayed outside the ring his punishment was over. Every shocked muscle and nerve of him wanted to quit. What was left of his reason told him to quit, that this was senseless. Why should he let himself be beaten to a pulp to satisfy some mysterious grudge of Dade's?

But something else deep inside him drove him grimly forward. At a stumbling run he crossed the line and by sheer momentum bulled his way to the center of the ring. He swung right and left at Dade with all his strength, knowing that it was hopeless. He felt the hammering begin again. Only this time it had shifted to his ribs and each blow was like a knife stuck into him. At last, on wobbling legs, his arms dangling helplessly at his sides and his mouth gaping, he stood and watched Dade measure him for the knockout.

He could not even close his eyes. He actually saw the twitch of Dade's shoulder muscles as the blow started. But it never landed. Dade too dropped his hands and stepped back. In a low, hoarse voice, he said, "I promised myself if I ever got the gloves on you I'd beat you till you whined. And now I can't even put you away. . . . Why don't you quit, you gold-plated dude, you?"

Before Hank could answer, another voice cut in: "Good afternoon, gentlemen. Am I interrupting something?"

Both of them started and turned. They had been too intent on their own affairs to detect the approach of a third person. Now they saw, sitting tall on a tall horse, Forest Ranger Crawford. He spoke quietly, almost casually, but Hank and Dade realized instantly that he was in such a rage as made their anger childish.

# FIVE

~~~~~~~~~~~~~~~~~~~~~~~~~~~~~~~~~~~~~~~~~~~~~~~~

## *Lookouts, Man Your Towers*

THE afternoon sun gleamed on two golden bodies polished with sweat. Within a circle of churned up turf they stalked each other, their gloved hands flicking in and out like the heads of snakes, faster than the eye could follow. Suddenly for a brief second, they seemed to melt into each other and the sound of leather on flesh was like beating on a wet drum. Then they sprang apart and the stalking began again.

To the ordinary person, it would have appeared that the two boxers were evenly matched. But the lone spectator was not ordinary. Unsuspected, he sat his horse in the shadow of the smokechaser cabin and watched. It was plain to him that the tall, towheaded young gladiator was making full use of his superior size and strength while the smaller, blackhaired one was the more skillful. Altogether it was a fierce and splendid contest, though a bit incongruous against a background of peaceful forest.

As if at a signal the boxers dropped their guards and stepped back. In a quick panting voice, Jim Dade said, "Dude, I'm telling you for the last time, don't drop your right while you're working your left. You uncover your jaw and if you do it again I'll tear your head clear off."

"O.K. Fair enough," returned Hank, and they squared away once more.

But the ranger interrupted by riding forward. "A man never knows what he'll come across on a trip around this ranch," he said pleasantly. "Sorry to break up the game, but I'm in a hurry and I want to talk business with you two for a minute."

Hank and Jim followed Crawford into the cabin. Dade was actually pale with terror. If he hadn't been a bit frightened himself, Hank would have felt sorry for him and amazed at the idea of Dade's being afraid of anything. Both of them were puffy about the lips. Hank's nose and Jim's mouth were bleeding and sweat continued to run down their faces in streams.

Blandly the ranger ignored their discomfort. He had already pulled a fistful of records out of the table drawer and was reading. For five minutes there was dead silence. At last he shook the papers together, put them back in the drawer, and looked at his two uneasy subordinates.

He said, "Your records are well kept and up-to-date. I'm pleased with the work you've accomplished. I don't recall any previous season when two lookouts managed to put the whole of Puzzle Basin in order without any outside help. It means you've been working together. There's no other way you could have done so much."

Hank and Jim drew their first full breaths since Crawford had appeared. But the ranger's voice seemed to harden as he continued, "My last visit up here was accidental and I found one of you two looking as if he'd run into a buzz saw. This time I came on purpose, because I wasn't satisfied with things. I was prepared to make some drastic changes. And I find both of you all beaten up."

His eyes swiveled around full on Hank. "Last time you told me that Dade was giving you boxing lessons. Is that still the explanation for all this gore?"

"Yes, sir." Hank spoke up promptly. "And I've improved a lot in a couple of weeks. I stood him off for three full rounds."

"Yes, I can see you've learned a few things. That left of yours is a thing of beauty." The tension went out of the room. It was noticeable that Crawford did not put Dade to the question. In this world there are a few people who know when to keep out of some-one else's business. "I withdraw all my doubts about the situation here," the ranger continued. "And I have some important news for you. You'll get it over the phone at report time, but I might as well tell you now. The fire danger is up to 4 and a lightning storm is moving our way. Tomorrow morning you'll man your towers."

# S I X

## *First Fire*

JIM and Hank stood before the Puzzle Basin cabin.
Already it had an empty look, for everything was put
away and the door was locked. Their packs leaned
against the wall. It was the end of three strange weeks
for Hank, and they had been anything but happy
weeks. Though he knew he had learned much, he had
a feeling of futility.

Here and now the trail which had brought him and
Dade together forked. Except to hear each other over
the telephone or meet by accident on the way to a
fire they would not see each other again this summer,
perhaps never. It troubled Hank that so far as he
could tell he had not gained one inch in Dade's esti-
mation. Somehow it had become very important to
win Jim's liking, or at least his respect. Young, eager
to please and inexperienced in the ways of the world,
to Hank failure meant that Dade had detected some
weakness in him.

Dade stooped to his pack and with one expert twist settled it on his shoulders. All at once he spoke, as if some pressure inside him forced the words out. "I suppose, because you saved my job with that song-and-dance about boxing lessons, you think I owe you something?"

Hank looked at him in amazement for a moment before replying, "No, I don't think that, Dade. As a matter of fact, I just couldn't admit that a guy fifteen pounds lighter and three inches shorter could beat me up. Besides, you did teach me to fight, so we're even on that deal."

"With a year's training, I wouldn't want any part of you in a ring," mumbled Dade grudgingly.

"But I'll tell you something you do owe me," Hank continued.

"What's that?"

"Ever since the day we met back there at smoke-chaser school, you've acted as though I had a small-pox sign hung on me. But I never saw you before in my life or did anything to you, and I want to know what your beef is."

"And I'll tell you," blazed Dade. "Did you think an ignorant hillbilly wouldn't spot you? You forget I was here last summer. You're a senator's son and a rich guy besides. Political pull and money to get you anything you want, including a job in the Forest Service."

Dade's black eyes sparkled with anger as all the words that had been bottled up inside him for three weeks poured forth.

"Did you ever wonder why I can box? Well, this is why: because I can earn the money with my gloves to pay for the education to be a forester. Did you ever earn your next meal or a place to sleep or the books to study with in a barn or a poolroom at five bucks a round?"

Hank simply stared at him, unable for once in his life to think of a thing to say. Dade apparently did not expect it. In a moment he ground more words between his clenched teeth. "I admit you aren't quite the panty waist I took you for. Because of that I'll put you wise to something. You got in here on your old man's dough and rep. But if you stay, it'll be on your own, because there's one guy in the world that can be pushed just so far. Crawford's putting you on Slide-rock, the point that makes 'em or breaks 'em. You'll have to spit the silver spoon out of your mouth and get some iron in your soul up there."

With that he spun on his heels and stalked off. In

a few moments he had disappeared into the forest. Hank shrugged into his own pack and automatically his feet carried him along the trail to Sliderock. How often in the past weeks he had looked at that trail and studied it on the map, longing to be on his way. Now he did not even see it. His thoughts were turned inward as he strove to see himself with Dade's eyes.

The trail was a good place to think, as many a man had discovered before him. But it brought little comfort to Hank Winton. Piece by piece he went over everything that had happened since his letter to John Stemple. He wished there were someone to talk it over with, and for a while his mind explored this sidetrack. Who could talk about it fairly? Not his father, who would naturally take his side. Not John or Crawford. A guilty conscience might be bothering them. For some odd reason the face of Dorothy Crawford appeared before him and he heard her saying, "I think you can eat in the same room with us, Hank."

She at least had not thought he was riding into the Forest Service on his father's name. But the picture faded. He could not escape the facts: his letter to Stemple, Crawford's telegram, smokechaser school, assignment to Three Rivers, and now Sliderock. It seemed to him that Dade had spoken the bitter truth.

Sliderock! Hank halted in the middle of the trail. He was going to the hottest point on the Forest. Even Dade couldn't read political pull into that. Hank squared his shoulders and marched forward. He could still believe in Stemple and Crawford. He marched grimly, no longer a knight going on a quest, but a man going to a hard and dangerous job. He had learned many things from Jim Dade—and paid a high price for them.

The trail to the lookout veered away from the canyon. It climbed among the mighty boles of spruce and tamarack. These were replaced by the slim trunks of lodgepole pine and they in turn by stunted scrub pine and mountain cedar. At last the trail emerged above timberline. Ever steeper, it traversed a gigantic, boulder-dotted slope.

At close range, Sliderock was less impressive than when seen from a distance. It became simply a mountain, mightier than its brothers, but still a mass of earth and stone. Hank climbed, his muscles carrying him swiftly where ordinary men would have had to pause and gasp every hundred yards. He did not regain the unearthly feeling of his first glimpse of Sliderock until he began to climb the stairs of the tower.

It stood on spidery legs, high above the broad sum-

Sliderock stood on spidery legs, high above the broad
summit of naked rock

mit of naked rock, and it swayed in the eternal wind. Dizzy, almost sick, Hank wondered briefly what the builders gained by adding twenty feet to the thousands already below him. But as he climbed he saw that the tower's height was exactly calculated to let him look down into the timbered canyons lying under the shoulders of the mountain.

He would have liked to pause on the catwalk of the tower for a long look around. The panorama was so vast that he felt stunned, unable to take it all in with one pair of eyes. But there was no time for daydreaming. The duties of a lookout when he first enters his tower are carefully set down in the "Smokechaser's Bible" and Hank knew them by heart.

He went first to the telephone and closed the switch. When he plugged in his headset he was rewarded with the ringing hum of a "live" circuit. He rang the Three Rivers call. In his mind's eye he could see the control room at the ranger station with Ben Gray, the dispatcher, surrounded by his maze of radio and telephone equipment. Each lookout line rang a bell with its own distinctive note and on a bad day the dispatcher's corner was sheer bedlam. But no one had ever heard Ben raise his voice or seen him lose his calm.

Hank's fingers had barely left the crank before the singing wire brought him the cool response, "Three Rivers."

"Winton, reporting in on Sliderock," said Hank.

"O.K., Sliderock," came the reply. "Check your tower and come in again. Hurry." There was just a hint of urgency in the last word.

Methodically, Hank went on with his task. He raised the shutters and understood why they were painted green on the underside when the brilliant light of that high and dustless altitude streamed in. Now the tower was revealed in all its stark simplicity: a glass box set on stilts. In one corner there was a small stove; along the opposite wall, an iron cot. In the exact center of the cramped room a pedestal held up the firefinder, the most important part of the tower.

A large brass ring was mounted over a map of the area that could be seen from Sliderock. On this ring were engraved the three hundred and sixty degrees of a circle. Above the ring was a movable sighting bar, with the eye-piece at one end and a vertical hair at the other. It was actually a giant compass. By lining up the sighting bar Hank could tell the direction of any fire. By reading the map under the firefinder he could tell the direction and distance. A simple device, marvelous when you understood what it could do.

While Hank worked he had also been listening. His headset cord was long enough so that he could stay plugged in wherever he went inside the tower. One by one he had heard the other lookouts report: Jim Dade's growl from Minaret; Brad Davis with a joke from Wildrose. Gray Plume and Scalplock he did not recognize, but there was no mistaking the rich Scandinavian baritone of Hjalmar Sorensen on Copper Mountain. It was comforting to think of those others, miles away, yet close enough, through the magic of electricity, to talk to and work with. Into his mind popped a name for them: the League of Lonely Men.

The telephone box under the firefinder jerked him back from his daydream by ringing his own call. The voice of Ben Gray followed: "Hello, Sliderock. If you're set up, I have a job for you."

A fire, before he had been in his tower ten minutes! Hank gave one startled glance around the horizon. "Sliderock ready for business," he said.

"O.K. Here's the dope, then. That lightning storm has passed us up. But it hit the next district. One of their lookouts is asking us for a cross bearing. Line up your firefinder on an azimuth of thirty-eight degrees and see if you can pick up a smoke at about ten miles. Minaret, you and Copper Mountain can come in on this. Minaret's azimuth five degrees; Copper Mountain, three."

With hands that shook uncontrollably, Hank adjusted the sighting bar. He peered through the eyepiece and saw that the hairline divided the upthrust of a distant ridge. Then, to gain a wider angle of vision, he looked over the sighting bar. In the sparkling air, mountain range behind mountain range stood out clear and sharp. But he could see no telltale plume of blue smoke.

"No reading from Minaret," snapped Dade's voice in his earphone. "There's a mountain in my way."

"Ay pick op smuk betveen tree ant zix," sang Hjalmar Sorensen.

"Well, that's something," Ben Gray remarked. "But it's no good for a cross bearing; angle of intersection too small. How about it, Sliderock? Have you got a reading yet?"

"I can't pick up a thing," admitted Hank unhappily. "Not a thing."

A faint edge appeared in the dispatcher's voice. "Something's wrong. You're only half as far away.

Check your azimuth, Sliderock, and search on both sides of it a few degrees."

"Maybe he's lined up on the backsight," jeered Dade.

Hank was getting confused. He verified the setting of his firefinder and knew in his heart that it was correct, the hairline riding above thirty-eight on the big brass scale. But there must be something wrong. He whipped out the binoculars his father had given him and stared until his head swam. But he could see no smoke.

"Well, Sliderock, what do you say?" asked the earphones.

"No smoke," reported Hank, unhappier than ever.

"Nuts!" said Ben Gray quietly but fervently, and there was a snort from Dade.

"Now vait a mannut," came the rich brogue from Copper Mountain. "Ay tank t' yong faller is right. Dat area is blind to him."

There was a pause and relief flooded over Hank. "Could be at that," said Gray as if talking to himself. "We'll do what we can with what we've got. Stand by, all."

A minute passed and another. In the earphones, Hank could hear several voices. They were very faint, but he thought he could recognize Crawford's. Then Gray spoke to him: "Sliderock, we're sending you on this deal. The best we can give you for a location is Section 20, Township 7 North, Range 1 East. Your azimuth 38 cuts it right in half. Check your map and give me your route and estimated travel time."

This was better, this was action. Hank glanced at the map under the firefinder. He said, "I'll take the lookout trail down the mountain, leave it at the six-mile board and go across country on azimuth thirty-eight. According to what I can see from here, it's open most of the way."

"Sounds O.K.," approved the dispatcher. "How about your travel time?"

"I figure three hours," replied Hank as he reached for the man-killer hanging beside the door. The weight of it was good on his shoulders, his caulks bit firmly as he scrambled down the tower steps. He felt supremely confident.

Three days later, footsore, grimy with sweat and dust, half-starved, he trudged wearily up those steps again. It was late afternoon and the sun was in his eyes as he pushed open the door and turned to ease the man-killer from his cringing shoulders. Then he jerked round in astonishment as the pack was lifted off bodily.

"Light and set a while, smokechaser," said John Stemple. "Looks like you'd put in a rough shift."

"Yeah," croaked Hank and grinned feebly. "What're you doing up here?"

"Came up to mind the tower while you were gone."

Hank nodded understanding. Exhausted and drooping as he was, he did not seem to be quite the same person. There was a new air of maturity and self-reliance in the way he spoke and moved. He said, "Guess I'd better report to HQ."

"Let it wait," replied Stemple evasively. "I saw you coming up the mountain and reported you in. Cranked up a mess of grub for you, too. While you're eating, I'll look over your Form 592."

Hank's fatigue-dulled eyes came to life as he saw the heaping plates. Obediently he handed over the crumpled, closely written Fireman's Report and attacked the food. Half an hour later, fed, washed and rested, he lounged with John on the cot while the afterglow stained all the tower windows red. It was good, he thought, to be a forester.

Abruptly, Stemple said, "Your report's O.K., Hank, except that you didn't put in the location of the fire."

"Couldn't," replied Hank. "It was off my map."

Curiously Stemple asked, "When did you eat last?"

"Yesterday about this time."

"How about water?"

"Got a drink at the spring on the way up the mountain. Before that not since last night. Found a little snowbank. Ate it, dirt and all." Hank spoke in matter-of-fact tones. Inwardly he was aching for a word of praise, not for the hardships but for finding the fire.

"Tell me a little more about the deal," prompted John.

"Well," said Hank carelessly, "when I got to the location the dispatch gave me, there wasn't anything. But I could smell smoke all right. Figured out that the wind was carrying it around the mountain. Took me quite a while to sniff my way to it, though. Met the lookout from the other district. He went home the second day; said he daren't stay out any longer. Fire was in his quadrant too, a big old snag, burning inside."

Into a few bald sentences he had compressed the story of his dogged search for the "lost" fire, the weary miles of following that elusive scent of smoke through brush and thicket and swamp, over windfall, ridge and cliff. He had persisted beyond the edge of his map, where his only compass had been that pungent odor in his nostrils. But Hank knew that Stemple could fill in all the details for himself and felt that his reward was sure. Hopefully he waited.

The alternate ranger's sober young face was outlined against the fiery sky and his lips were set. He understood only too well what Hank had been through, baked by day and half-frozen at night, tired and discouraged, at the last without food or water, but sticking to the job with the splendid loyalty of youth, youth that never knows when it's licked. For some reason there was a lump in his throat that he could not swallow.

Grimly at last he said what he had to say. "Hank, you went out to find a fire and you found it. Nobody can take that away from you. But there's more to it than that. You were gone three days and we had no idea where you were or what you were doing. You've got to remember that you're part of an outfit and you and the outfit have to keep track of each other. As a matter of fact we were about to send out search parties when I spotted you coming in. That would have tied up most of the men on the district. When a man doesn't report at least once in twenty-four hours we figure he's in trouble and the outfit gets ready to back him up. D'you see what I'm getting at?"

"I guess so," admitted Hank ruefully. He had let John Stemple and Crawford down and his world was crashing about him, but he did not show it. "I could have reported; I passed a couple of telephone lines. Just a one-track mind."

"Don't take it like that," urged John. Something warned him that his words had gone deeper than he intended. "You did a one-hundred percent job. You just didn't think out all the angles. No one expects you to right off the bat. You know, there's no substitute for experience."

John laid a hand briefly on his young friend's shoulder. "Well, I've got to head on down the mountain."

Hank kept up his brave front until Stemple had gone. Then he dropped down on the cot again and stared blindly at the darkening sky. He ached in every muscle, his feet were blistered and his shoulders chafed, but these minor pains did not register in his mind. He was thinking that no matter how John tried to smooth it over he had met his first test as a forester and failed miserably.

~~~~~~~~~~~~~~~~~~~~~~~~~~~~~~~~

## SEVEN

## *Storm*

DISTRICT RANGER CRAWFORD re-
turned to Three Rivers from an inspection trip of his
own on the morning after Stemple's return from
Sliderock. The ranger's eyes took in the scurry of
activity which never ceases around a wilderness headquarters, identified it as normal and went on to a
little glade beyond the corrals. There, with Dorothy
Crawford as interested spectator, John was "whip-
breaking" a tall, high-spirited black horse.

"Whip-breaking" is the old horse trainer's term
for teaching a horse never to stray far from his master
and to come at a call or even a motion of the hand. As
practised by John, a whip played no part in the teaching whatever. His equipment was a lariat rope and a
long coil of fish-line plus infinite patience and understanding.

As Crawford approached he could see that the
lesson was about over, with Dorothy taking the part

of trainer and the horse apparently enjoying himself as much as anyone. Seeing her father, Dorothy came to meet him, leading the glossy animal by the forelock, he ambling along behind and every few steps giving her a playful nudge.

"Isn't it marvelous?" she asked. "Isn't he good now? I can ride him now, can't I?"

"If John says so," replied the ranger.

"He's all right now," asserted Stemple. "Never was anything wrong with him except a knot-headed horse breaker somewhere along the line. All he needed was to be understood."

"Evidently," remarked the ranger. He looked significantly at his daughter.

"Oh, sure," said the girl. "You want to talk business, so 'run along, will you, Dorothy?' . . . It's a conspiracy." Obediently she went off across the meadow with the horse prancing beside her.

"Tell me about Hank," said Crawford abruptly.

John told him the story of Hank's first fire, leaving out nothing. "Poor kid," he concluded, "he was out on his feet when he got back to the tower but still going."

"Kids are wonderful," agreed the ranger. "That

word 'quit,' they never heard of it. I'm sorry for one thing, though."

"What's that?"

"I'm sorry you jumped on him for not reporting in."

Amazement wrote itself on John's face. He protested, "But Boss, I couldn't let it go. I never hated anything worse than having to climb on him. But you can't let a thing like that go."

"John, my boy," said the ranger, "there's such a thing as having too much conscience. That lad put out everything he had for us, came in on his last legs, believing he'd done a good job. Would you do that to a horse, ride him half to death and then give him a kick in the belly because he bumped your leg on a tree? You would not; you'd give him a currying and a big feed of oats and you'd go to work on his faults after he'd rested up."

John's eyes strayed across the meadow where he could see the "outlaw" he had just finished training following Dorothy like a huge, frolicsome puppy. His face was miserable.

"Yes, you can take that horse as an object lesson," continued the ranger inexorably. "I never saw anyone so easy with horses as you and so uneasy with men."

"I see it," admitted John humbly. "All I could think of was the book and the page and paragraph. Hadn't I better get back up there and try to undo the harm I've done?"

Crawford shook his head. "He'd see through you in one second. It's a ticklish proposition. What we've got to do now is give him a chance to get back his self-confidence."

"You're right," admitted John. "But if I've messed things up for Hank, I'll—I'll——"

Crawford laid one great hand on his shoulder and shook him gently. "Relax. It isn't as bad as all that. . . . I know, we'll let Dorothy go up to see him. She's the best little morale builder on this ranch."

John left, visibly relieved, and unaware of the lines which appeared in the ranger's face the moment he was out of sight. In his own mind Crawford was worried about Hank. He had that rare gift of understanding which allowed him to see with another man's eyes, feel with his nerves. It made his crews fanatically loyal to him even while they called him "slave-driver" and "man-eater." The result was the most high-powered firefighting organization in the northwest— and haunted dreams for the ranger. Only too clearly he understood how a person like Hank, worshipping John as he did, would magnify and distort John's mild reprimand. And there was so little he could do about it. Between a single individual and a million acres of wilderness he had no choice but to let the individual fight it out as best he could.

On Sliderock, minutes passed into hours, hours became days and days, weeks. Life became as harshly monotonous as the ticking of a watch. Hank crawled out of his iron cot at daybreak, the sun tipping the Wolf Cub peaks with fire while the canyons were still in darkness. It was always cold at this hour. He touched a match to the fire already laid in his stove. Then he made his first inspection of his "Circle." This took fifteen minutes, a slow circuit of the tower while his eyes combed each canyon, mountain slope and ridge. By the time he was done the energetic little stove had driven the chill outside the glass walls and his coffee pot was bubbling. He had breakfast, washed his dishes, swept out the tower and made his bed. This took twenty-three minutes.

Eighteen minutes with axe and saw were enough to replenish the fuel he had used up the day before. Now came, for him, one of the best times of the day. With a five-gallon waterbag on his back, he made a trip to a spring—a mile and a half down the mountain, a mile and a half back. Many a lookout managed on a gallon a day, but Hank had a dislike for stale water and besides the trip did something to satisfy his craving for company. On Sliderock's naked summit there was except for himself no living thing, not even a hardy shrub or tuft of grass. But the spring was a meeting place for all the creatures who made their homes on the lower slopes of the great mountain.

He was certain to find the tracks of deer, elk and mountain goat in the wet sand. Often he met them face to face. He even came to recognize individuals, like the old billy goat, patriarch of his tribe, posed motionless on a rocky outcrop. Hank could never resist laughing at his absurd beard. Or the monster bull elk with the white scar along his ribs and his horns in velvet who gave up his place at the spring with stiff-legged disdain. In time they apparently came to recognize him, for even the shy deer no longer ran. They merely moved off to a safe distance and stared at him as if wondering what this outlandish creature on two legs might be doing on the mountain.

Once he was lucky enough to surprise a mother

grouse and her brood of chicks at the spring. With the heart-breaking courage of her kind she put herself between him and her young ones and strove to draw him away by pretending she was crippled. Hank had to wait half an hour for his water that day, until with much clucking and fluttering the hen had led her flock off. The tiny balls of fluff were invisible against the ground except when they moved and Hank was afraid he might step on one. But ordinarily, loiter as much as he would, the excursion was over in an hour and twelve minutes.

In the time between his return from the spring and eight o'clock, Hank checked his instruments and records. He tightened telephone connections, tested the night light over the map-board, sharpened pencils and polished the firefinder which needed no polishing in the dry and dustless atmosphere. Promptly at eight the lookouts all reported to headquarters, starting with Hjalmar's singing baritone from Copper Mountain and proceeding in a great circle around the district. No one had a name. It was "Copper Mountain, visibility twenty-five miles, gentle south wind, sky is clear and no smokes; Minaret, visibility twenty-five miles, gentle south wind, sky is clear and no

smokes; Sliderock, visibility . . . wind . . . sky . . .
no smokes." It was as if the men had been absorbed
by their towers.

After all reports were in, Ben Gray, the fire dispatcher, gave them the weather forecast, the fire
danger for the day, and any special instructions. Then,
by unwritten agreement, the lookouts could gossip
for an hour on their party line. It was against regulations but Crawford was no slave to "the book" and
he knew what a relief it was to the boys imprisoned in
their glass cages to exchange jokes and cooking recipes and gabble about anything under the sun.

"Better to have them talk nonsense to each other
than start talking it to themselves," he had once told
a regulations-conscious inspector from Regional
Headquarters. And into his mild tone he had managed to put the implication that if the inspector
didn't like it he knew what he could do. Without
taking any part in it, Crawford often listened to "The
Peak Rats' Old Home Week & Debating Soci-
ety," as the lookouts called it. The earphones
brought him all the signs of taut nerves, suspense, fear
and doubt, of deadly routine and aching loneliness
which are the portion of the lookout.

He could tell almost to the day when some lad had

reached the breaking point. And no one was ever the wiser when that lad was suddenly but smoothly transferred to a different job, then to another until he eventually disappeared from the Service. The ranger was utterly ruthless about eliminating the unfit, but in his heart he went through the ordeal with each first-year man, cheering him on, helping where he could, cushioning the fall if a fall became inevitable. The sorry tale had never been told on Crawford's district of a lookout driven beyond his limit and sent away broken-spirited, or worse. But though he listened, he never heard the voice of Hank Winton during the gossip hour.

When Gray cut into the babble of voices with his cheerful, "All right now, you birds in your gilded cages, let's get down to business," the day really began. Fifteen minutes out of each daylight hour Hank spent searching his area for smoke. It was done according to schedule and the schedule of each lookout was cunningly fitted into the others so that five minutes was the longest any portion of the forest went unwatched.

The other forty-five minutes out of the hour, Hank could do what he liked—so long as he stayed within hearing distance of his telephone. He could study his smokechaser's bible and the few books he had brought with him, he could look after his equipment, he could try new recipes out of the smokechaser's cookbook. Like Jim Dade, most lookouts became expert cooks. And he could think.

But he did not think the thoughts he had expected to. During the months before he became a forester he had thought of this as a time for planning and dreaming great dreams. But now his mind went round in a dreary circle, like a bear on a chain. Crawford and John had given him a job because they felt that they owed it to him and his father. Dade had spotted him as a phony in a moment. And now it was proved by the way he had bungled his first fire.

During the first week, he had watched the trail daily for sight of someone coming to take his place. The second week he had prayed for a chance to redeem himself. After that he sank into a sort of apathy. He performed his duties to the last detail, but mechanically and without satisfaction. There was no elation for him in looking out over the magnificent spread of wilderness which was his to guard. He had already failed it once and undoubtedly would again. He listened to the other lookouts, often he heard them call to him with a "Haow's it agoin' way up thar on Sliderock, podner?"

They sounded so natural and happy that it made him cringe and he always gave a short answer, though he yearned for companionship. As the days passed, one idea grew stronger in his mind. John and Crawford were sorry for him. That was why he hadn't been jerked off Sliderock as he deserved. In that case, there was only one thing for him to do. He must resign.

"Resign." The wind that blew eternally over Sliderock whispered it to him. The sun glared it at him out of the brassy sky. The grim inner voice which is a man's conscience told him.

Nothing in particular happened to bring about a decision. It was an afternoon like any other. He had just completed his circuit of the tower. In his official diary he wrote: "4:55–5:10 P.M. inspected my area. Visibility good except for haze in the west. No smokes. Left the tower at this time in order to hand in my resignation."

Then, quite simply and calmly, he hung up his headset, stuffed his few belongings into his packsack, and went. But he descended the steps of the tower stumbling, as if in the dark.

At that same moment, events which had been marching slowly and by different paths suddenly picked up speed, joined and made a pattern. In the west, the haze which Hank had seen thickened until it was like a black curtain. At district headquarters Gray, Crawford and Stemple hung over a radio. As its chatter died away Crawford said, "That's it. Alert the district. Tell the fire chief I'll want a hundred reinforcements ready to move on call."

And Dorothy Crawford turned the head of her black horse into the trail that led up Sliderock.

Hank traveled swiftly. Now that the decision was made he felt better. The exercise warmed his stagnant muscles and quickened his nerves. He might be a failure as a forester but at least he was honest enough to admit it. He stopped at the spring to drink and splash the icy water over his head. When he rose his eyes were bright and alert again. Action was a shock that roused his mind. Now he received another shock that woke it completely.

Where the trail made a sharp bend around a rock outcrop he suddenly found himself face to face with a horse and rider. It was so totally unexpected that he stood speechless, staring at Dorothy. And in that moment he saw completely and in its true colors what he was doing. He was quitting, deserting because another lookout didn't like him and because John Stemple had pointed out a mistake.

He was so ashamed and so angry at himself that he could only stutter when Dorothy called out a "Hello there, Hank."

Frantically he looked at his watch. He still had twenty minutes to get back before evening report time. To the girl he mumbled something about having to get to his telephone. Then he spun on his heels and without another word ran up the mountain like a startled elk.

Even as he sprang up the tower steps he could hear the telephone shrilling his ring over and over. He tore the headset off its hook, jammed the plug home and gasped, "Sliderock."

"Where the devil've you been, Sliderock?" demanded Gray. Then, before Hank could make any answer, the dispatcher plunged on: "Never mind that now. There's a sockdolager of a storm moving in. It will hit the district about dark. Get ready for night observation of lightning strikes. Wait a minute, here's something else."

Gray's even voice was replaced by Stemple's, rough with anxiety. "Hank, is Dorothy up there?"

"Not yet," replied Hank. "But she's on the way up the trail."

"No chance to head her off." John's voice was almost a sob. "Hank, she'll have to stay in the tower until the storm is over. Don't let her out on the mountain in it. Do you understand me?"

"Why sure, boss. We'll be glad to have her company." By "we," Hank meant himself and Sliderock. His hate and fear of the great mountain had gone along with his false reasoning and his doubts. Hank was himself again.

When Dorothy reached the tower, he was busy fitting a ring of white cardboard around the rim of the firefinder. In darkness except for the feeble mapboard light, he would not be able to read the azimuth scale. But he could take a sight on each lightning bolt and mark it on the cardboard. Then, by day, he could get the readings.

"Well," said the girl, "I must say you have a funny method of greeting a visitor. You look at me as if I were a ghost and then run like mad. I didn't know it would be that big a shock."

Hank, with his yellow hair falling over his eyes, grinned at her apologetically. "I shouldn't have been out of the tower," he explained. "And the dispatch was tearing the telephone to pieces when I got back. Here's a shock for you. You have to stay up here until this storm goes by."

Unexpectedly Dorothy began to laugh. "For two years I've begged my dad to let me ride out a storm in a tower. And he just looks at me as if I'd said 'Let's invite the Regional Forester over to play leapfrog.' Now he tells me I have to do it." Abruptly her face sobered. "But my horse!" she exclaimed. "He can't stay out there. He'd be killed. I can make it off the mountain if I start right away."

"No soap," said Hank. "Orders are orders. We'll turn the bronc loose. He'll go home all right."

Together they descended from the tower. The black horse, with mane and tail streaming in the wind, came up and nibbled Hank's arm in friendly fashion. Hank tied up his reins and fastened the stirrups so they wouldn't flop. "G'wan, beat it," he ordered and waved his arm threateningly.

The black horse thought he was playing. He pranced off and then back again. He nudged the girl, plainly asking her to mount and leave this windy, grassless place.

"It's no use," said Dorothy. She was almost crying. "John trained him too well. He won't go."

But Hank hadn't spent the best part of a summer with that horseman without learning a few of his tricks. "I'll fix it," he assured the girl. He stripped off saddle and bridle and gave the horse a slap on the thigh. Free of his badges of servitude, the black understood. With a snort and a series of exuberant kicks, he took the trail off Sliderock at a gallop.

The peaks were stained an angry red as Hank and Dorothy put away their supper dishes. Together at the west window they watched the storm approach. The haze of early afternoon had become a curtain, the curtain had become a cloud. A stupendous wall of cloud with towering battlements, it loomed bold and clear against a blue-black sky. The sun went down and a few pale stars appeared over the tower. To the west they winked out one by one, devoured by the cloud as it seemed to devour all earth and space. The familiar rustle of wind at the eaves of the tower took on a whining note.

"I thought it would be exciting," said Dorothy. "It is, and more than exciting. It's—it's too big to talk about. I'm scared."

"So'm I," admitted Hank. "But we're all right as long as we stay under our protection." He showed her the thick copper conduits leading to the ground from the lightning rods on the tower roof. Even the cot and the stove were connected to this metal web.

A spark glowed briefly at the underside of the cloud. Much later came a long, low growl. Hank had begun counting "ONE and TWO and THREE" with the flash. He stopped at the first sound of thunder and figured briefly on a bit of paper. Then he rang headquarters. "Sliderock reporting," he said. "Picked up lightning at twenty-five miles. I'm going to start taking strikes."

From then on the advance of the storm was incredibly rapid. As it came closer, they could see that the cloud was veined with constantly shifting lines of crimson. The lightning shafts it threw at the earth were much heavier, and at times they quivered in the air for whole seconds before blinking out.

To begin with, Hank took readings only on the heaviest strikes and Dorothy read the compass scale. But they were not too busy to be awed by the majestic and savage power of the storm.

Dorothy said suddenly, "It doesn't seem possible that a flimsy thing like this tower can stand up under such a beating."

"They do it, though," retorted Hank. "There are half a dozen of them doing it right now."

At that moment a tremendous flash lit the sky. It died, but as if it were fighting back, a red glare spouted up from the earth. Hank laid the sighting bar on it and began counting seconds. "Oooooh, that was a dirty one," he breathed. "The flareback means it started a fire for sure. Azimuth 274, distance fifteen miles, let's see where that might be."

He strained his eyes in the dim glow of the mapboard light, checking off the miles with one finger. Then, quickly, he lifted his hand and swung the sighting bar. But he was too late. Dorothy too had seen where his finger stopped, on the triangle within a circle which, on Forest Service maps, means a lookout tower.

"Direct hit." Hank began to talk hurriedly and jerkily, as if by explaining he could drive the stark fear out of Dorothy's eyes. "You see, these ground cables have to end in water or they can't carry away all that juice. Sometimes a spring dries up and nobody notices and then—— Poor devil," he concluded lamely, "it wouldn't last long."

Grimly he went back to work. Thunder was almost continuous now and it came in sharp, rending cracks that rattled the glass walls. The wind had become gusty, wrenching savagely at the tower. And now the storm seemed to be just outside, walking toward them on legs of lightning.

Hank reported to headquarters for the last time. Then he hung up his headset and threw the switch that grounded the telephone. A lightning bolt struck the far edge of Sliderock's summit, and turned into balls of fire which bounced crazily in every direction. A ghastly radiance lit up the tower. Sound battered it, sound so tremendous that it was like a silence.

"Here we go," said Hank and his voice was a thread. "Better sit here on the floor beside the firefinder. Got to keep as far away from metal as possible."

Obediently Dorothy huddled against the wooden pedestal. "You too," she said faintly.

Hank shook his head and pointed at the firefinder to explain that he must mark as many of the strikes as possible. He felt her pulling at him and bent down until her lips were against his ear.

"If we don't get out of this, I want you to know you're a swell guy, Hank Winton." She shouted the words and he barely heard them.

Terror had him by the throat but he shouted back, "We'll go through."

Lightning struck the mountain in half a dozen

places at once. Through the bellow of thunder came a sharp crackle from the roof and for an instant the copper conduits glowed red hot.

There was a moment's pause, as if the storm were gathering itself together. Hank looked down at Dorothy and in the eerie light saw that her eyes were closed. Her face was calm and her lips moved steadily. He bent down and heard:

"Our Father, Who art in Heaven——"

Lightning ripped all across the summit of the mountain like a fiery knife.

"——Thy kingdom come, Thy will be done——"

The tower shuddered as the next bolt crashed directly upon it and sheathed it in fire.

# EIGHT

## Second Fire

THE lightning storm departed even more rapidly
than it had come. The flashes became scattered and
less blinding. The thunder gradually sank once more
to a low growl. Incredulously, Hank and Dorothy
Crawford looked at each other, unable to believe that
they had come through such violence alive.

Then for a time they were slightly hysterical. They
walked around the tower stiffly, as if their muscles
ached. They laughed at everything, the sickish sweet
odor of ozone, the fused and melted end of one of the
ground cables dangling from the ceiling, an empty
ration box which Hank had left on the catwalk and
which had been reduced to a handful of charred sliv-
ers, none over an inch long.

"Lightning proof, that's what they call us," giggled
Dorothy.

Hank regained control of himself first. He built a

fire in the stove and made coffee. Over the steaming cups they grew calmer.

"I suppose they'll be worrying about us," suggested the girl at last. "Do you suppose the telephone still works?"

Hank replied, "Guess it's safe to find out, anyhow. You know, these lines carry enough induced current to knock a guy clear out of the tower while a storm is on."

Gingerly he threw the switch. There was a frantic jangle from the bell and then a voice clattered in the earphones: "——hottest storm I ever rode out. Some tower west of us burned and I saw Sliderock take five direct hits. Maybe I'd better go over there." It was the voice of Jim Dade and for once he sounded worried.

That Dade could be anxious about anyone was surprising; that Dade was anxious about him was incredible. Then, with the strange exhilaration of the storm still throbbing in his veins, Hank broke in: "This is Sliderock. One ground cable burned out but everything else is O.K."

Gasps of relief from several different people came over the noisy circuit, followed by the unmistakable voice of the ranger, hammering out each word as sharp and clear as new coins: "Sure glad to hear from you, Sliderock. Your visitor can start down the mountain at daylight. Thanks for looking after her, Hank. In the meantime, start working up your fire data. We've got a busy day coming."

Hank turned to Dorothy with a smile. He felt oddly triumphant. It was really the tower which had fought off the storm. But he felt like part of it now. He was about to make some joking remark when the expression on the girl's face brought him up short. She was holding his Forest Service diary.

"Hank, what's this?" she asked with horror in her voice.

For a moment Hank was puzzled. He looked at the diary and then the elation drained out of him like blood from a wound. "Left the tower at this time in order to hand in my resignation." Had he really written those words? He could scarcely believe it now, but there it was in his own hand. He looked at John Stemple's girl with sick eyes. Of all people in the world, the first one to learn that he was a quitter had to be John Stemple's girl. His head sank lower and lower.

When Dorothy spoke again her voice had steadied and it carried a note of confidence and understanding that lifted Hank's head like a magnet. She said, "I'm so glad I saw this first. Those idiots down at HQ might take it seriously. But things like this look bad on the record." With a quick wrench she tore the entire sheet out of the diary and before Hank could move, she had stuffed it into the stove.

"It doesn't change anything," said Hank. "I'm still a dirty quitter."

Dorothy laughed at him. "That's a funny way to quit, by riding out the hottest storm that ever hit Three Rivers on the hottest point in the district. You had plenty of time to leave after you knew a storm was coming in. . . . I tell you what, I'll make a little deal with you. I'll keep quiet about your having a brainstorm, and you keep quiet about my sitting on the floor saying my prayers. Or would you rather I took a skillet and beat some sense into you?"

Hank still had a sense of humor. The mental picture of Dorothy, half his size and weight, beating sense into him with a frying pan was too much. He began to laugh in his turn. "O.K.," he said. "You win. It will be a couple of hours before it's light enough for you to pull out. How about helping me work up this fire data?"

With the girl holding a flashlight and writing down

the figures, Hank began to translate the marks on the firefinder into directions and distances. He never noticed how behind his back Dorothy dabbed at her eyes with a handkerchief. Born and raised in the Service, she had seen other young foresters driven to the edge of despair. Knowing what John and her father thought of Hank, she whispered another prayer: that she had done and said the right things to save him for the Forest.

Hank had no time to think about the events of the night. Dorothy left in the first gray light of dawn. Fifteen minutes later a transport plane droned by, flying so low that Hank could look in through its windows and see the cabin crowded with men. The pilot dipped his wings as he passed the tower and then tilted the plane's nose down for the long glide to the Three Rivers landing field. And this was only one of the signs that the Forest Service was marshalling its forces against its ancient enemy.

The first rush of traffic on the telephone was over, but there was a constant clatter in Hank's earphones of lookouts calling in new fires. He had reported on nearly fifty "smokes" himself and his eyes told him that there must be many more beyond his visibility range.

Headquarters, he knew, must be sheer insanity. There four other telephone circuits and two radio nets came together. All would be chattering their own tales of disaster. But it was planned and orderly insanity. These were the critical hours when in the still air of morning each fire sent up its individual plume of smoke. Soon they would merge into one impenetrable cloud of vapor under which the red legions would march to the destruction of the whole forest.

"Hello Sliderock," said Ben Gray. There was nothing in the dispatcher's unhurried voice to tell that he had already been on duty for twenty-four frantic hours. "What looks worst to you up there?"

Hank was ready for him. "My No. 12 on azimuth 39 is throwing up a lot of black stuff," he said professionally. "I put it in Section 5, Township——"

"Yeah, I've got it. We have a good cross-bearing on that one from Minaret. His azimuth is 8 and the fire's in the northeast quarter. You'd better take that one——"

"What's the idea?" snarled Jim Dade suddenly. "That fire's in my quadrant."

"Pipe down, Minaret," said the dispatcher impatiently. "We've got something figured out for you.

Sliderock, take that fire. It's in a dirty place so give us a fast run. You're on your own."

"Good luck, Sliderock." The earphones called that after Hank as he went out the door and he could identify the voice of Sorensen.

So many things had happened to Hank in so short a time that part of him was numb. His lungs tasted the invigorating air, his legs felt tireless as steel, his eyes and ears were alert. But he felt no emotion whatever, no eagerness, no dread, not even curiosity. He was going to his second fire and he went as casually as if it were only to the spring for his daily supply of water.

His route to the fire was simple, at least to him, knowing the use of map and compass. At a certain switchback far down the mountain he took a compass reading and then struck out cross-country. For several miles he followed a line that existed nowhere except in his own brain. It was straight in the sense that he moved from one landmark to another which, on the map, could be joined with the edge of a ruler. But his path on the ground was a maze of curves and tangents and detours. He had to avoid impassable cliffs and mountain bogs. He scrambled in and out of ravines; he plodded through forest so dense that he was in twilight and never saw the sky for minutes at a time.

But from alpine parks, from the crests of ridges, once from a treetop, he could see the tower on Sliderock. A glance at his map, a quick compass sight on the tower, and he knew just how to turn to get back to that invisible line which led from Sliderock to the fire. In a different quarter of the horizon, Minaret loomed up as another beacon. He had not been able to see the smoke of his fire since he left the mountain. It was masked from him by forest and tumbled ridges. Now his compass told him that he was close to the intersection of the two lines of sight from Sliderock and Minaret. Science had done all it could for him. He was in a labyrinth of ravines and ridges, all heavily wooded. The rest would depend on his woodscraft.

He began to circle like a hunting dog, sniffing the vagrant air currents. On his second circuit, he found the fire.

"Hello, fire," he said. It seemed a perfectly natural thing to do as he took off his man-killer and got ready to fight.

At headquarters, Crawford looked at Stemple with undisguised amusement. "You'd give a year's salary, wouldn't you, to beat it over there and see how your boy makes out?" he teased.

"Let me go," begged Stemple. "A look at the fuel map is enough to tell you he can't handle that alone."

"Not very romantic, are you?" chided the ranger. "There's our girl friend, Dorothy, somewhere up around Puzzle Basin with no horse, and you want to go rushing off after some smokechaser."

John had his mouth open for a hot retort, but caught himself in time, warned by a lift of one eyebrow. "What've you got up your sleeve now, boss?" he asked.

"Almost got you," chuckled Crawford. He appeared completely detached from the hurly-burly around him, men coming and going, telephones and radios gabbling, pack-trains loading supplies and equipment at the hitch rail, airplanes roaring on the meadow. It was an attitude born of complete confidence in the firefighting organization he had built. He had done all he could. Now the fate of a million acres of wilderness lay in the hands of a few tens of smokechasers, each making his lonely way to a red dot on his map. Knowing each of them, Crawford could relax.

He continued, "Hank's got a rough little fire on his hands. He can't corral it, but there's a trail crew on the way to back him up. He can stand it off until they get to him. The point is, I intend to see this one in person. I've got to have some of the fun around here." With that he went outside, mounted his horse and rode away, leaving John to gape after him.

Crawford, with the trail crew which he had picked up on the way at his heels, reached the fire in the late afternoon. He and the crew foreman scouted it together. To their practised eyes it was plain what a desperate and losing struggle had been fought in the area.

"He really put up a fight for it," said the grizzled old foreman admiringly. "Well, we'll mop up the flanks and tackle the head when the sun goes down. It won't get far now. This smokechaser did the hard part. Wonder who he is?"

"Wonder where he is," replied the ranger in a puzzled tone.

At that moment one of the crew men called, "Hey boss, you'd better come look at your smokechaser. He's passed out."

Sharp fear stabbed the ranger's heart. In firefighting there was always the unpredictable; a sharp tool swung carelessly, a puff of wind when a tree was almost ready to fall, a rolling log.

He found Hank lying face down at the end of the

Hank was lying face down at the end of the fire trench

fire trench he had been building. His pulaski was still gripped in his hands and his shovel leaned against a tree near by. The fire had eaten right up to the long scar of naked earth and then gone on uphill. Only a smokechaser's luck or some last instinct of self-protection as he went down had caused Hank to drop outside the fireline. Beyond that narrow barrier, the fire still smoldered sullenly amongst the roots of blackened trees.

Crawford, kneeling beside him and fumbling for the first-aid kit in his pack, could see no sign of any injury. His fingers found the artery in the boy's wrist, felt the pulse, light and far too rapid. He turned Hank over on his back and saw his face, pale beneath its grime and clammy with cold sweat. Hank's open eyes were blank as glass, but it seemed to the ranger that they followed him with a desperate question in their depths.

"Now just take it easy," said Crawford. "Twenty-five men are after your fire."

"What happened?" It was the merest thread of a whisper.

"You can read all about it in your manual tomorrow," replied the ranger cheerfully. "It's called heat exhaustion, plus a little smoke and a whole lot of trying too hard. You darned kids never know when to holler 'Whoa.' "

Crawford poured aromatic spirits of ammonia into water and held it to the boy's lips. Then he disengaged his fingers from the pulaski. They were so stiff that he had to unbend each one separately. He began to rub them between his own calloused palms.

Ten minutes of the ranger's expert care brought Hank back to full consciousness, though he was still weak and sick. Twice, while moving him to a more comfortable position, Crawford held him while he threw up violently. Even his retching smelt of smoke.

"That's the stuff," the ranger encouraged him. "Get all that poison out of your system. . . . Now, d'you feel enough better to tell me about this?"

Crawford thought he had never seen such despair in any eyes as the boy replied, "There's nothing to tell. The fire got away from me. You can see that." Helpless tears rolled down his cheeks.

"Careful now, or you'll lose him," the ranger admonished himself. It was not the first time he had seen a firefighter hysterical from exhaustion and defeat. Hank had literally fought until he dropped; the signs of that fight were all around for any practised eye to read. And he had lost, which was worse than the poisons he had breathed and the hours of killing toil.

Aloud Crawford said, "Don't let a fire getting away bother you. It happens all the time."

"Quit kidding me," grated Hank. "I messed up my first job. You gave me a fire that belonged to Jim Dade so I'd have a chance to make up for it, and I let it get away. I've been a washout ever since I came here and you and John can't prop me up any longer. If you won't can me, I'll do it for you. I'll quit."

The shrug of the ranger's broad shoulders said that it was just one of those things. "If your neck's bowed for it, I wouldn't argue with you. Often thought myself a man must be crazy to pick this way to make a living. That reminds me, though, your old man is somewhere in the country, heading for Sliderock to see you. I'll radio John to head him off."

Hank's dull eyes brightened momentarily at mention of his father. Hastily, the ranger continued, "Anyhow, before you pull out you've got to complete your Form 592. Just give me the dope and I'll put it down."

Deftly he extracted the paper from Hank's shirt pocket and spread it on his knee. He began to write and talk at the same time, apparently unconscious that he, not Hank, was telling the story of the fire. "I see you arrived at 10:43 after a two-hour run. That puts it in the danger period of the day right off the bat. The fire started in a lightning-struck tree. When you got here it had a perimeter, including spot fires, of three hundred yards.

"You found some patches of dry brush beginning to blaze up and throw sparks, so you dirted them down first. Then you laid out a fireline that would take in all the burning area, a better proposition than trying to corral a dozen small fires separately. But you couldn't watch everything at once and some spots got across your line.

"The wind was beginning to pick up and burning conditions were in high by that time. You knew you had a tough proposition on your hands. You backed off and looked it over. In order to do any good you figured you'd have to get a line across the whole front of the fire. That meant giving yourself some leeway and, of course, the fire a chance to link up and get on a head of steam.

"Well, it was a chance you had to take. You moved ahead about a hundred feet and started your new line. It was tough digging and that pulaski all of a sudden weighed about fifty pounds. But you just about had your line finished when some young trees in amongst the big stuff began to crown. You went in there and cut them down and killed the flames with dirt. But while you were doing that the wind pushed the main fire around the end of your line.

"You decided you should have been twins, or maybe even triplets. And you couldn't remember anything they taught you at smokechaser school to cover a deal like this. In school, the smokechaser always wins—they call it psychology. You could see you had about as much chance of corralling that fire as a forester has of getting rich. More trees were beginning to crown and the fire was working into a belt of second-growth stuff, dry and flammable enough to blow up if you looked at them.

"You figured you might be able to keep the fire on the ground, though. So you tackled those trees, got your eyebrows singed off and your lungs full of smoke. But it was no go. The fire got up and made a run for it and you had to back out or be fried.

"Right there is where nine out of ten firefighters would have called it a shift. You'd stood the blasted thing off all day. Evening would be along with cooler temperatures and less wind. And sure as anything some lookout would have reported that there was an awful lot of smoke coming out of this gulch, so there'd be help on the way.

"But you had one shot left. No use to let the flank of the fire widen out. It was burning slowly enough so you could do something with it. That's what you were doing when you keeled over."

Hank had been following this reconstruction of the fire with gradually increasing interest and amazement. When the ranger stopped talking, he exclaimed, "How do you know all that? Were you here?"

"Didn't have to be," retorted Crawford. "It's written all over the ground, one of the doggonedest fire-fights ever put up in these parts. We like to keep men that'll fight, too. But you figure we poured it on you and I don't blame you. Because we did and would again tomorrow."

This outrageous misstatement had the desired effect. Hank sat straight up with eyes blazing. "I never figured any such thing," he protested angrily.

The ranger managed to look puzzled. "I must not be very bright today," he said. "I thought there was a beef about giving you another man's fire."

"No!" Hank practically shouted it. "I let the fire get away and I said I wouldn't let you and John cover up for me any more. I want to stay, I'd give anything to stay, but I'm—I'm——" Hank was getting confused.

"Oh, that," said the ranger as if he had just managed to get things straight in his mind. "We never did think you could corral this fire. It had too much headstart on you. But we figured you could stand it off until a crew got here, which you did. That's the sad fate of smokechasers, my friend. You go out and take it on the chin all alone. Then, when the tough part's over, some brass-bound ranger turns up with a small army and grabs the credit."

It brought a grin to Hank's pale lips. His mind, dazed by exhaustion and defeat, was beginning to focus again. He said hesitantly, "You mean I—I did all right?"

"One hundred per cent. . . . Well, I want to give this 592 to the crew foreman and see how he's getting along. You take it easy until I get back."

Crawford was gone three-quarters of an hour. When he returned, Hank had disappeared. With a wide grin of satisfaction Crawford read the note he had left: "I'm heading back to Sliderock. Feel O.K. Tell my dad I'll be looking for him."

# NINE

~~~~~~~~~~~~~~~~~~~~~~~~~

## *Perfect Gift*

HANK WINTON had been through a mental and physical ordeal that would have put an ordinary person in the hospital. But he had a mountain-trained body, tough as latigo leather, and the incredible recuperative powers of youth.

He had a slight headache and was a bit unsteady on his feet. Both of these after-effects of the fire disappeared before he had covered a mile on his way back to Sliderock. His legs, the smokechaser's yardstick of how much more he can stand, lacked their usual spring and drive, but they carried him smoothly.

A city dweller walking in the mountains has to pay attention every instant to what he is doing or he will find himself scraping pine needles out of his face or traveling in a circle. But a forester develops an automatic homing compass in his brain and eyes and feet. He marches along, thinking his own thoughts and observing all the interesting things that go on in the wilderness.

Hank had much to think about. For so long a time he had thought of himself as a failure. He had looked on his second fire as a final test. Every ounce of skill and strength he possessed had gone into fighting it. Then, as it seemed to him, after toying with him for most of a long and bitter day, the fire had brushed him aside as casually as a moose brushes aside a tuft of willow.

Then the ranger gave him a completely different picture, of a battle fought with cunning and determination, a battle lost before it started so far as he was concerned, and yet won because he had delayed and thwarted the enemy until help came. It was not possible to doubt the ranger, face to face, but it was hard for Hank to readjust his ideas. With all his might he clung to the new belief that he had done a good job. There was a solid glow of satisfaction in it like nothing he had ever felt before.

Hank was going through an experience which comes eventually to every young "punk" fighting his way up in the Forest Service. He was beginning to see himself not as a lone individual matching his puny strength against the forces of Nature, but as a member of a team. He had actually seen for the first time how beautifully it could function, the whole power of the District closing up behind the lone smoke-chaser. When he looked at it that way, the fact that the smokechaser had taken a beating was of no importance at all. That's what smokechasers were for.

It all boiled down to one thing: just let anyone try to keep him from going back to Sliderock now.

While these thoughts went through his mind, Hank's legs carried him along at the forester's steady three-and-a-half-miles-per-hour cross-country pace. His eyes systematically quartered the wilderness for whatever might be worth seeing. Presently their arc took in a ridge parallel to the one he was following and picked out a moving speck.

There was no mistaking the outline of a smoke-chaser's packboard with the shovel and pulaski handles projecting at the top. Another smokechaser was homeward bound after his own ordeal by fire and it seemed to Hank that the swing of his broad shoulders and long arms was familiar.

Two people spying each other across the immensity of the wilderness are irresistibly drawn together. The paths of the two smokechasers gradually swung toward each other. For minutes at a time they were out of sight, but each reappearance found them closer together. At last, as casually as if it were the corner of Park and Main, in the twilight of a grove of immense alpine spruce, Hank came upon Jim Dade.

A few days ago, even a few hours ago, he would have traveled miles to avoid such a meeting. Even now he was a little uncertain. His belief in himself was still new and unfamiliar. He dreaded a sneer from the black-eyed lookout more than fire or lightning. Yet something drove him forward too, as if he could never rest until he had proved himself to Dade.

"Hello, Jim," Hank said. "Long time no see."

Dade tossed a handful of huckleberries into his mouth, replying at the same time with a grunt. A few weeks in a lookout tower had evidently not loosened his tongue much.

"What kind of a fire'd you draw?" asked Hank.

"Grammar school stuff," snorted Dade. "Just a little trash burning. Nothing to it." A spark of curiosity lit up his soot-black eyes. "Quite a bit of smoke coming out of your spot when I left the tower."

"Yeah. It got away from me too along about the middle of the afternoon," admitted Hank. "Crawford showed up with a crew and it's corralled now."

In his own sudden and unpredictable way, Dade

exploded. "Got away from you! What d'you think you are, a twenty-five man crew with trenchers and pumps? And the old man showed up on it himself, did he, so you could strut your stuff in front of him? You lucky stiff, you. Well, I can't stall around here all day chewing the fat. Be seeing you, dude." He hitched his pack up higher on his shoulders and was off without a backward look.

You could trust Dade, Hank thought, to punch from an unexpected angle. He had been braced for insult or mockery, even indifference—anything but envy. But Dade had a way of going straight to the heart of any subject and it was something to have made him envious. Hank wondered if he would ever really understand Jim.

Slowly he made his own way out of the grove and climbed to the top of a ridge. Across a canyon which was already a lake of darkness loomed the fantastic bulk of Sliderock. Its crown still glowed warm in the sunlight and the windows of the tower were a golden blaze. With a lifting heart, Hank set out on his long climb to the sun.

In his own quarters at Three Rivers, the ranger was going over the day's collection of fire reports with John. Unheeded by either, Dorothy kept their cups full of coffee and their plates supplied. They were still dusty from the trail, fatigue had clawed lines into their faces. But they talked and ate and wrangled in a way that could only mean good news.

"A hundred and fifty fires down and out," said the ranger, riffling the reports. "Only four extra-period and three still burning. Only one Class C. I tell you, it's one for the books. What a bunch of smokechasers we've got around here!"

"Not surprising," remarked John solemnly. "You've only spent ten years kidnapping them from every district between here and the Coast Range."

"Lower your voice when you say things like that," pleaded the ranger in mock alarm. "But look, I haven't told you about your protégé yet. Honestly, that kid beats anything I ever saw. He fought that fire of his until he collapsed from exhaustion and smoke. And then what do you suppose?"

"I don't suppose, I want to know," replied John anxiously.

"He wanted to quit his job because the fire got away from him, after standing the blasted thing off single-handed all day. How d'you figure the lad ever got into such a frame of mind? We've worried about him a time or two—all these kids have to be watched their first season, until they learn the ropes. But I never looked for anything like that. He really had me floored for a while."

"Well, but what did he finally do?" asked John.

"We talked the thing over and I left him resting up while I had a look at the fire. When I got back he'd pulled out; left a note saying he was going to his tower. Say Dorothy, call the dispatcher, will you, and ask him if Hank has reported in yet?"

"I did and he has, twenty minutes ago," replied the girl.

"Boss, how much longer do we dare keep this up?" The worry lines were carved deep in John Stemple's forehead.

"Keep what up?"

"I mean—that boy is tearing himself to pieces. I— I almost think sometimes we ought to put a stop to it, for his own good. He tries too hard."

"Now there you go again," snorted the ranger. "You and your one duckling. Get it through your head that every man is entitled to fight his own private devils and all his friends can do is egg him on. You, of all people, ought to know about that."

John's rare smile lit up his face. "O.K., boss. But I

wish I knew the names of some of those devils. I'd like to take a poke at them."

The two left for the office to listen in on the late weather reports. Dorothy, watching them go, smiled after them with a wisdom and tenderness beyond her years. "Private devils," she murmured. "A lot you know about them."

On Sliderock, Hank was shoveling the last bites of an enormous meal into his mouth with one hand and holding a letter with the other. In Senator Winton's characteristic scrawl, which only he, Hank and his secretary could decipher, the letter said:

"Dear Son,

Why don't you foresters ever stay at home? I drag my weary bones to the summit of this unmentionable mountain to see you and you are off on an azimuth, whatever that might be.

In any case, please put out all the fires right away. I came here to fish, not peel potatoes as I did all last summer, and I didn't care for the look in Mr. Crawford's eye during my brief but pleasant visit with him. Incidentally, he tells me that you are showing at least rudimentary aptitude in forestry.

*That pleases me, although I confess my inability to understand why anyone should want to be a forester. I prefer to remain a dude and go fishing.*

*When you are done playing with fire, let me know via our mutual friend, Ben Gray, who undertakes to forward your message, and we'll have another go at getting together. For some mysterious reason I'm anxious to see you, you young oaf. Meanwhile I am leaving with you as substitute for myself an article which I am sure will be more amusing and even more long-winded than I am.*

*Your Father"*

It seemed to Hank that the Senator's pungent personality still lingered in the tower. He could almost hear his father's acid comments as he puffed up to this lofty and fishless altitude. What fun it would have been to show him the tower and explain its equipment, to astound him with an apple pie and teach him the smokechaser's lingo. It was something to look forward to. And now irresistible curiosity led him to the mysterious carton which held his father's gift.

From the moment he had come into the tower he had wondered what it might contain. Buying a present for a lookout would be something of a problem. Books, perhaps, or one of those collections of cakes and candies; possibly a plaid shirt. Something to read, eat, or wear. There was little else a lookout could use. Cautiously Hank pried the carton open, for the Senator had what he called "occasional attacks of the lowest form of humor: the practical joke." But the box contained nothing that jumped, made thick smoke, bad smells or loud noises. With bulging eyes, Hank lifted out the newest, finest and most powerful model of portable radio.

"Pop, you're terrific," he said aloud.

With trembling fingers, he extended the whip-type aerial. He clicked the switch and the stars rained music. A twist of the tuning knob and the glass walls spoke to him of the great world beyond even his vision. In the presence of that magical companion, one at least of a lookout's private devils could not exist. Loneliness, that corrodes a man's soul and distorts his mind, was banished from Sliderock. The Senator had chosen the perfect gift.

As Hank sat entranced before his radio an idea came to him. Quickly, before the objections could daunt him, he acted upon it. He rang headquarters on the telephone and explained his great idea to Ben

Gray in words that stumbled over each other in their eagerness.

The dispatcher turned to Stemple and Crawford, who were poring over a lengthy Forest Service radio message that had just come in. "Excuse me for interrupting you gents," said Ben in his usual humorous drawl, "but I think we'd better sweep out the padded cell. Sliderock has flipped his lid. He wants to broadcast to the other lookouts."

Crawford and Stemple blinked at him with the dazed expressions of men suddenly jerked out of the depths of a knotty problem.

Hastily Gray went on to explain: "He says his father left him a portable radio. He thinks by holding his telephone transmitter close to it he can send over the lookout wire net. Want to let him try?"

Crawford was the first to recover. The effect of Hank's plan on him was startling. He sprang out of his chair and prowled the cramped little office like a tiger, his eyes blazing.

"By all the red gods of the wilderness!" he roared. "Ten years I've beat my brains out trying to figure ways to make it a little easier for those poor, miserable devils on the towers. And now a kid who shaves only once a week has to show me how. Will I let him try?

Why, if it doesn't work I'll make life a burden to every electrician in the Forest Service until it does work."

Ben translated this outburst to Hank: "The boss says to go ahead, Sliderock. I'll get all the maniacs on the line, then you take it away."

Tensely Hank listened to the emergency ring. One by one he heard the far-scattered lookouts report. When the last was in he said, "This is Sliderock, all you peak rats. I've got a radio up here, uh—a friend of mine gave it to me. I'm going to hold my transmitter close and try to let you in on it. Stand by."

He tuned the radio carefully, turned up the volume and put the mouthpiece of his headset in front of the speaker. In his own earphones he could hear the river of music flowing out to the League of Lonely Men.

At headquarters, the ranger sprawled in his chair, a picture of pleased contentment as the harmonies of a famous dance band poured out of Ben's earphones. Stemple brought a frown to his face by mutely holding before his eyes the radiogram they had been studying.

"Yes, yes," growled Crawford. "I remember. We've just licked the most fires in the shortest time in history. So what do the brass pull out of their hats?

All they want is to snatch the guts out of my organization and send them to some godforsaken district that can't fry its own fish. Well, they can wait an hour. This is history too."

When Hank turned off his radio an hour later the wires promptly became a babel of voices: "Don't stop now . . . more . . . how about a newscast? . . . Keep it going, Sliderock."

Ruthlessly Ben Gray broke in, "Pipe down now, you lookouts. Station Sliderock will be broadcasting again soon—we hope, we hope. Now listen to business. Hank Winton and Jim Dade report to Indian Battleground at once for special duty. Your reliefs are on the way. Don't wait for them. Start now."

# TEN

~~~~~~~~~~~~~~~~~~~~~~~~~~~~~~~~~~~~~~~

## *Roll Out Or Roll Up*

ALL the long way down from the mountain Hank puzzled over the meaning of this new and unexpected development. There was something alarming in the fact that he and Dade had been called together. Could their old quarrel be rising out of the past to plague them now? Hank had never flattered himself that the ranger was at all deceived about the two "boxing matches" he had witnessed. But then there were those words "special duty" at the end of Ben Gray's message. They might mean anything. They might even be a polite way of saying that two Three Rivers lookouts were in serious trouble. The only certain thing was that a lookout led a hectic life. Nothing happened for weeks and then everything happened at once.

Half-hypnotized by the beam of his headlamp, Hank plodded along the trail. He was so tired now that even his brains felt like putty and it took an effort of will to keep his eyes open. In the midst of worrying about what might be going to happen, he knew that he was beyond caring. Dade, with his gift for boiling everything down to essentials, would have a word for it: punch-drunk.

Near the base of the mountain a spark of light came up the trail to meet him. Hank exchanged a few words with his relief, an utter stranger to him. The man knew no more about what was going on than Hank. He was tired himself and grumpy at being called out in the night. They soon parted.

Dade, with a shorter distance to travel, was already at Indian Battleground when Hank arrived. He had a fire going and a pot of coffee on the stove. They shared this in a sort of glum companionship. Hank was dizzy with fatigue and the edges of Dade's iron temper were blunted. The usual surly contempt was missing from his voice as he denied any knowledge of what was up.

He dismissed the subject with a shrug and the forester's phrase for the inexplicable: "They said there'd be days like this—and then they'd get tougher."

At the station no one was stirring besides themselves. Hank reported to Three Rivers by telephone.

In response he got from Ben Gray a cryptic, "O.K., Hank. Stand by for further instructions."

The minutes went by and the two smokechasers nodded over the stove, half asleep. Simultaneously their heads came up. Some faint vibration in the air had penetrated the fog of their weariness. It grew and became recognizable. A plane was drumming up the valley of the Wolf. Now it was overhead, a gigantic bat figure against the starlit sky. It dragged the wilderness landing field once with two great red eyes staring down and then settled on earth, its exhaust stacks vomiting fire.

Roused from their lethargy, Hank and Dade stumbled out to it, reaching it just as the active figure of John Stemple dropped out of the dark cabin. "Hop in, you two," he shouted over the racket of the idling motors.

Obediently they climbed aboard and made their way forward toward the vague figure of the pilot silhouetted against the glow of his instrument panel. The moment Stemple slammed the cabin door, the engines howled and the plane began to sway over the bumpy meadow.

Stemple put his head close to Dade's and Hank's.

"We're going to help out a Forest that's in trouble over west some place. I don't know exactly where. You birds had better get what sleep you can. It looks like one of those things."

It should have been wildly exciting, this night flight to the rescue. Hank tried to tell himself that he was excited, that this was adventure with a capital A. He was conscious of the brief pressure of John's fingers on his shoulder, a whole volume of greeting in a touch. For the rest he was numb. He saw Dade snuggling down on a heap of cargo parachutes and fell into place beside him. He was asleep almost before the plane was airborne.

Of the flight hundreds of miles west over mountain, river and forest, he knew nothing. It seemed to him that he had barely closed his eyes when the jouncing of the plane woke him up and told him that they had landed again. His eyes felt sticky, but there was life in his legs again as he stumbled after John and Dade toward the beacon of a lighted window in a strange ranger station.

They entered a typical Forest Service headquarters. Except for the slightly different arrangement of telephones, radios, map boards, and filing cabinets, it could have been Three Rivers. In the harsh glare of an overhead light they blinked at the sole occupant of the office. He was small and slender and appeared to be shrunken inside his smudged and dusty Forest-green uniform. He was even more gray-faced and red-eyed than his visitors, yet the invisible mantle of authority lay upon his drooping shoulders.

Stemple said, "Party from Three Rivers, Ever-green Forest, reporting. I'm John Stemple, this is Jim Dade and this is Hank Winton."

"Ah yes, Crawford's men." The words came slowly as if each one had to be forced through a barrier of exhaustion. "I'm Supervisor Hardy of the Saca-jawea Forest. Can't tell you how glad I am to get hold of any part of Jack Crawford's outfit. I'm also ashamed to have you find us on our knees, but these things happen. What kind of shape are you in?" The tired eyes had evidently been busy.

Stemple glanced half-apologetically at his companions. "We're bent a little," he admitted, "but not broken. Give us the dope and we're ready to go."

A smile briefly erased the tragic lines in the Supervisor's face. He said, "That's all you ever get out of a Three Rivers man, isn't it? 'Ready to go.' Well, here's the situation in one word. We're swamped, especially on this district. The ranger here got smoked up and is in the hospital. His alternate was hit by a snag—still unconscious, poor fellow. The dispatcher is a good man but green. He's out now trying to scout our worst fire. You can see what we're up against. We have sufficient manpower but a critical shortage of leaders.

"I've got a job all picked out for you, a fire I've had to leave in charge of civilians up to now. It doesn't seem to be doing much but I can't get any satisfactory information out of those people. Stemple, you'll take over there as fire boss. There's a base camp and two fire camps out. Winton and Dade will take over as foremen. Here are your maps and such reports as have come in. You'll find a car in the garage, and food in the kitchen. Don't go out on empty stomachs."

After a hasty meal, Hank felt almost normal again. He was experiencing that miraculous ability of the human body to tap hidden reservoirs of energy. With the car bouncing over a rough wilderness road and the cool night air pouring in at the open cab windows, he began to feel excited for the first time. The same process was working in his companions.

"What does the deal look like?" asked Dade.

John replied, "Can't really tell till we look at it.

The reports are a joke. But it's a queer set-up. They have two twenty-five man crews out on a two-hundred-acre fire burning in a stand of mature white pine. Looks a little top-heavy. That stuff doesn't ordinarily burn very fast unless it really blows up and there's no indication of anything like that. It's on level ground and they've even got a Bosworth trencher."

"What kind of a Forest is this anyway?" grumbled Dade. "Crawford would handle that with one smoke-chaser and a cook's flunky."

"Take it easy," advised Stemple. "It's kind of tough to lose the two tops out of a district, bang, bang."

"I feel sorry for that supervisor," remarked Hank. "Never saw a guy that looked any sicker."

"He's entitled to look sick," snapped Dade. "The Sacajawea—why, that's the center of the white pine belt, the finest saw timber in the West. If he burns it all up, the brass will have his hide, and that's for sure."

"You talk like a radical," chuckled Stemple. "The brass isn't that bad. You've got to remember they have higher-up brass tailing them. But this supervisor's got his hands full, all right. This thing we're on is two-for-a-nickel. He's got a plus-thousand-acre fire we'll probably look over before we're finished. I saw the reports before we left home."

The tents of the base camp were ghostly in the headlights as they reached the end of the wilderness road. Stemple wasted no time waking anyone. He checked maps with Hank and Jim and started them up the trails to the fire camps. And he paid them the supreme compliment of letting them go with a minimum of advice. All he said was, "Let's get this cleaned up quick. There are bigger fish to fry. I'll be along to see you as soon as I get strung out here."

As he followed the glow of his headlamp through the woods, Hank's mind was in tumult. The others seemed to take the whole affair as a matter of course and he had tried to be as casual. But to be a lookout one hour and a fire foreman a few hours later was beyond his wildest dream. He was frankly scared by the thought of trying to command twenty-five firefighters. What would he say to them? What would he say to the foreman he was replacing? That gentleman would hardly appreciate waking up to the news that he was out of a job. Suppose he refused to recognize Hank's authority? Furtively he touched the forester's badge on his shirt pocket. That must be his talisman.

In that pallid hour just before dawn, when the

pulse of every form of life is at its lowest ebb, Hank reached his fire camp. Actually he almost walked right through it without knowing that he had arrived at his destination. He thought, "There's something the matter with this picture."

There is nothing elaborate about a fire camp: a tent for supplies, another smaller one to serve as a headquarters, perhaps a fly over the camp kitchen. The men sleep in the open, for in rainy weather there is no need for firefighters. He could see their ungainly figures, swathed in sleeping bags, lying at random among the tents.

It was all wrong. At this hour forest fires too burn low. The camp should have been a beehive of activity, the men fed and ready to start for the fire line. And there wasn't even a pot of coffee on the sheet-iron cookstove. Pure instinct led Hank to the headquarters tent. Inside he found a giant of a man, bearded, dirty and fully clothed, snoring away on his back. Hank had never felt younger or more inexperienced than when he looked down on the man, formidable even in sleep, whom he had come to replace.

It took all his resolution to shake him into consciousness and tell him, "I'm taking over this camp,

Supervisor Hardy's orders. I'm going out to scout the fire and when I get back this crew had better be rolled out or rolled up."

This was a set speech made up on the spur of the moment, and Hank thought it a masterpiece, especially the last line. In forester language "roll out or roll up" meant roll out of bed and get to work or roll up your personal belongings and leave. He did not wait to see its effect. In the gathering daylight his eyes confirmed what his nose had already told him, that fire was near. He found it on the other side of a low ridge, a vale where lordly trees showed like ghosts through the blue haze of smoke.

It would have been a terrifying sight to the uninitiated. Hank instantly recognized a fire that was traveling slowly along the ground, smoldering really. The great trees were motionless and soundless but Hank could sense their agony as the red death ate among their roots. To think that the crew, his crew, was at the camp asleep when every man should have been here, fighting for the lives of the trees, made him angrier than he had ever been in his life.

When he returned after a brief survey of the fire, he found that the camp had wakened. One man was sullenly poking twigs into the flaming maw of a cook-stove. The rest, headed by the giant from the tent, were in a disorderly group, plainly waiting for him. He walked up within ten feet of the leader and halted. No little speech occurred to him now and the bald antagonism in the foreman's eyes sent little shivers up and down his spine.

"You the guy that woke me up and told me you're taking over?" demanded the giant. Hank noticed how wet and red his lips were, like a wound half hidden by the tangle of hair that matted his cheeks and jaws. "Well listen, you Forest Service punk, I was logging this country when you were getting your meals out of a bottle. I was hired to put out this fire and I furnished the crew. And me and the boys figure on doing it our own way. Now beat it, Forest Service, before I pull that pretty badge off your shirt and shove it down your throat."

Hank had heard stories of people like this logger, people who would deliberately prolong a forest fire for the sake of days of extra pay. But until now he had never believed them. All the anger that had possessed him when he scouted the fire came rushing back. But it was a different kind of anger. That had been hot and quick. His anger now was cold and calculating. No one who had ever known him before would have recognized good-humored, friend-of-all-the-world Hank Winton now. His head was down between his shoulders, his chin against his breast, and his eyes glared with icy fury. His arms hung twitching at his sides and he swayed back and forth, balancing on the balls of his feet.

"You're fired," he told the logger in a grating voice. "You and your crew. If you aren't out of here in five minutes, I'll throw you out."

Without a word of warning, the logger charged. Hank had known he would before ever the man moved a muscle. His hands were already in fighting position, the left half extended, the right cocked just in front of his chin. The logger seemed to come in slow motion, his every action as plain as headlines in a newspaper. As Hank danced to meet him, he remembered one thing Jim Dade had drummed into him over and over: hit at a target. Not just the face or body, at a bull's-eye: the mouth, the point of the chin, or that vulnerable nerve center, the solar plexus.

Hank had already chosen his target. He moved his head a fraction of an inch and the logger's wild swing went harmlessly over his shoulder. Then Hank hit him on the nose six times with his left, so rapidly that the sound was like one blow.

The logger stopped in mid-rush as if he had run into
the end of a pole

The effect was startling. The logger stopped in mid-rush as if he had run into the end of a pole. Blood spurted over his face. With an animal cry of pain he clapped his hands to the gory mess. For an instant only; then with a bellow of rage he charged again, his arms pumping like sledge-hammers.

Hank circled now, moving to his left, and always his left hand licked in and out, always to the same mark. No creature of flesh and blood could stand that punishment, delivered not with padded gloves but with knuckles like iron. The logger teetered on his heels. He took one staggering step backward after another, his arms still flailing the air, even as Hank himself had once staggered back. For the first and only time in the fight, Hank unleashed his right hand. A twisting, gliding motion that began in his toes ended with the solid smack of an axe going into soft wood, as his fist went inches into the logger's midriff.

Calmly Hank stepped back, lowered his guard and watched his enemy collapse at his feet. Then he whirled like a tiger as a voice spoke behind him.

"Very, very pretty," said Jim Dade. "You didn't even drop your right. Man oh man, if I hadn't seen it, I'd have thought you'd worked that big galoot over with a pulaski." Suddenly Dade's voice became a roar. He stepped past Hank and faced the sullen, shifting mob of the logger's cronies. "Now, you timber lice, if you want more of the same, come and get it, one at a time or a dozen. If you don't, pick up your carrion and hit the trail."

It was nicely timed. The mob knew it could overwhelm two foresters, but each member of it winced away from the thought of his face beaten to a bloody pulp. Hank alone would have been swarmed under in another instant, but a pair of such foresters was too much.

Hesitantly two men came forward, stood the logger on his feet and dragged him away. In a shuffling herd, they all moved down the trail to the base camp.

Dade blew out his breath and said, "That was close. For a second I figured they were going to take us."

Hank all at once felt drained of strength and emotion. Ashamed, but helpless, he was violently sick to his stomach under Jim's curious gaze.

"I used to do that too, my first couple of fights," said Jim. "You get over it."

Hank was still too churned up inside to notice that Dade was talking to him in a tone he had never used before. "What'm I going to do now?" he croaked. "What'll Stemple say when my whole crew comes out of the woods?"

"Think nothing of it," chortled Dade. "I fired mine too. That's how I happened to come over to see how you were making out."

"Yours too?" parroted Hank. He looked dazedly round him at the deserted camp.

"Aw relax," snapped Dade with a touch of his old impatience. "We can beat this stinking fire out with our hats. Why there's a Bosworth trencher over in my camp. We'll have the thing on a mop-up basis in two hours."

He was right about it too. The ground where the fire was burning was level, at least as level as ground can be in the mountains. There was little underbrush and the lordly white pines were rather widely spaced. The situation was made to order for a Bosworth trencher. Two hours later, when puzzled and anxious John Stemple arrived from the base camp, Hank and Jim were wrestling the snarling, bucking little machine over the last hundred feet of fire trench.

Stemple listened to their report that the fire was now corralled and needed only patrol action while it burned itself out inside the trench. But if the two smokechaser-foremen had hoped to divert his attention from what had happened earlier, they were doomed to failure.

Abruptly John said, "I salvaged a few of those men you canned. They weren't really in the clique, just bull-dozed into playing along. They can take over the mop-up. I'll have to file a report on this go-around, of course. It isn't every day that fire foremen put the bounce on whole crews and then corral the fire by themselves. The first thing I want to know is this. Hank, did you really work that big logger over with nothing but your hands? He looks as if you'd run your Bosworth over him."

Hank, speechless with embarrassment, could only nod. Dade answered for him. "The guy swung on him. What else could Hank do?"

"Just what he did do, I guess," replied John. Then he asked curiously, "How long did this fracas last, anyway?"

"Thirty-three and one-half seconds of the first round, by the watch," stated Dade.

Stemple looked at Hank with a baffled expression. Squirming uneasily, with his hands down and fury no longer glaring out of his eyes, the tall young smoke-chaser looked like anything but the deadly fighting machine which had reduced a tough and experienced bully to a trembling hulk in a little over half a minute.

"I didn't know you were a fighter, Hank," said John. "How come?"

Hank found his voice at last. "Dade taught me— while we were working together at Puzzle Basin."

Stemple smiled at last. "Kind of a rough combination, you two," he said. "The way that riffraff came out of the woods I thought the fire'd blown up and was right behind them. . . . Well, let's get going. I've reported this fire under control and we're relieved. We have to go back to headquarters."

The trip back to the ranger station was made in almost complete silence. The many hours of continuous effort behind them were beginning to press on them like leaden weights. Hank dared not draw attention to himself by asking, but he thought that surely now they would rest and eat. He felt as empty as a drum and only the rough jouncing of the truck kept him awake.

Numbly, the three trailed back into the ranger station and stood once more in front of the Supervisor. To all appearances, he had not moved since their departure hours earlier.

He gave them a wan smile and said, "Quick work, even for a Crawford outfit. I thought there was something phony about that fire, but a man can get around to just so many places." For a moment he paused and eyed them speculatively. "What kind of shape are you in now?"

Even John's iron self-control seemed to be wearing thin at last. "Let's not play around," he replied shortly. "We need to eat and sleep. But we're still ready to go."

The Supervisor gave a dry little laugh. "I had no business asking you that, but I couldn't resist. Things are beginning to pick up a little; there's food waiting for you in the kitchen and beds upstairs in the bunkroom. But before you go after them I have one more question."

"Why doesn't the guy get to the point?" mumbled Dade in Hank's ear. His growl was drowned out by Stemple's asking, "What's the question?"

"This. In addition to your other accomplishments, do you three happen to be smoke-jumpers?"

# ELEVEN

~~~~~~~~~~~~~~~~~~~~~~~~~~~~~~

## *Ready to Go*

SMOKE-JUMPERS are the elite troops of the fire-fighting army. Few in number, specially trained and equipped, they spread their parachutes over the most inaccessible and roughest corners of the wilderness to fight fires that could not be reached for days overland.

Hank knew something of their history. How the bush pilots of the Forest Service first thought up the idea. How the invention, by Forest Service engineers, of the static cord that opened the jumper's parachute automatically and the jump suit had made the idea practical. Every earth-bound smokechaser called them "glamor boys" and thought of them with admiration and envy. After the storm at Three Rivers, Hank had even seen two of them jump on a fire, grotesque in the armored suits that protected them from rough landings among rocks and trees.

When the Supervisor of the Sacajawea National

Forest asked if the Three Rivers men were parachutists, there was a moment of dead silence.

"I can jump," replied Stemple quietly. "Dade and Winton, no. Why, what's the deal?"

"I'll say he can jump," thought Hank. He remembered only too clearly how John, without jump training, had parachuted into the center of the great Moose Lake fire the summer before and rescued a trapped crew.

"That's unfortunate," said the Supervisor. "I couldn't permit a man to jump alone in any case and this job requires at least three. I asked because all the regular chutists are used up."

Two voices in perfect unison blurted, "I'll jump," and Hank and Dade looked at each other in surprise.

The tired eyes of the Supervisor lit up but before he could say anything Stemple broke in. "Don't listen to the young punks, Mr. Hardy. They haven't had one second of jump training. It's absolutely out of the question."

With Hardy carefully taking no part, the argument lasted fifteen minutes. Point by point the two enthusiastic smokechasers beat John down. They had him in an awkward spot and made the most of it, harping on the fact that he had made his own first jump without training. There was nothing to it, they insisted. All you did was step out the door of the plane and let the ground come up to meet you. The Supervisor cheered them on with his eyes.

Wearily at last, Stemple turned to him and asked, "What is this job you've got for three bumbershoot men?" It was a tacit admission of defeat. Hank and Dade recognized it and were instantly silent.

"We have a conflagration on this Forest," explained Hardy. "A number of smaller fires that joined on us and then the whole business blew up. We don't even know how big it actually is now. Had to pull out all the crews and reorganize. I smell a chance to get it under control. The extended weather forecast promises favorable wind and higher humidity for a few days beginning tomorrow. I have the men and a lot of heavy equipment, bulldozers, pumpers and so forth, ready to go. If I only knew where the blasted fire is and what it's doing . . . Here, let me show you on the map."

He led Stemple to the large-scale map that covered most of one wall of the office. "My guess," he continued, "is that the front of the fire is working up the northern exposure of this range—and what a beautiful stand of timber that was! You see how steep the ground is on that side and how the southern slope is gradual? If we could meet it with our bulldozers along the crest, while the wind is from the south . . . You see what I'm up against, sending all those men and that equipment in on the head of a fire. I just can't do it without reliable information, and by the time we scout that fire on foot it will be over the ridge and off on another run."

"I see all right," growled Stemple. "All you want us to do is jump in front of that fire—*at night*."

"The moon is full," replied the Supervisor. It was the closest he ever came to pleading for his dying forest.

Stemple said, "If it was Crawford, I wouldn't be so surprised." His infrequent smile illuminated his drawn face as he turned to Hank and Jim. "You got us into this. Just 'step out the door and let the ground come up to meet you,' huh? What a rough education you're going to get. . . . Well, Mr. Hardy, the arrangements are up to you. Me and these young roosters, we've got some eating and sleeping to catch up on."

It was night again. On the landing field near the ranger station could be heard the idling motors of a plane. Well fed and rested, Hank, John and Dade were helping each other into their bulky jumpsuits, padded and reinforced to protect their bodies from the clawing fingers of tree branches. Around their waists went the heavy belts festooned with rope, axe and other equipment. The two parachutes were slung one in front and one in back. In his arms, each man cradled a tiny chutist's radio.

The pilot watched their preparations in aloof silence. With the adventure upon them, no one had much to say except "Cinch that strap up a little tighter" or "Got your map and compass?" The Supervisor fussing around them seemed to be the only nervous member of the group.

When they were dressed except for their wire-mesh face masks, he drew the Three Rivers men to one side, away from the noise of the engines. He said, "I'm having one crew with a bulldozer start breaking a way in from the south side at once. They will leave the road at this point and follow this high ground." He indicated the route on a map. "They'll be available in case—in case of any trouble. The main party will jump off as soon as we get a favorable report from you. I authorize you to abandon your parachutes and jumpsuits. And—and every man in the Forest Service is pulling for you tonight."

Awkwardly the three climbed into the plane and found themselves places to sit or squat. It was impossible to find a comfortable position, loaded down as they were. The pilot entered behind them and slammed the cabin door. Immediately the motors bellowed and lifted them into the night.

Once the plane was airborne, there was no sense of movement. The engines droned steadily, too loud for conversation. Hank looked at the dim bulks of his companions, monstrous and misshapen like creatures from some other world. He wondered what they were thinking. He himself was trying not to think or, rather, to think of anything but that moment when he must step out into space.

His best refuge was to go over and over the instructions for scouting the fire. He would jump first, at the eastern edge of the conflagration. Dade would go second, in the center, and John last at the western edge. Once on the ground they would make contact with each other by radio and then move out to spot the location, extent and rate of travel of the front of the fire. The pilot, hovering overhead, would listen in as they reported what they found and relay the information to headquarters over his more powerful radio. When the job was done, and it must be done quickly, they would make their escape to the south, converging on the route of the rescue party with the bulldozer.

"But what if one of us gets hurt?" Resolutely Hank drove his mind away from that thought.

After an endless time, Hank tasted smoke in his nostrils. As if that were a signal, John got up and waddled forward to a position just behind the pilot. Hank struggled up to his knees and looked out a cabin window, conscious that Dade was doing the same. He could see nothing. The plane was flying above the fire, swathed in clouds of smoke.

Suddenly then, the plane broke out into brilliant moonlight. To Hank's left the wilderness was outlined in pale radiance, streams, gorges, alpine lakes, mountains and forest. To his right everything was shrouded by impenetrable vapor. The plane was fly·· ing directly above a miles-long ridge, precipitous on one side, sloping gradually on the other. Comparing this scene with the map he had studied until it was printed on his mind, Hank got his directions straight. He knew where he was; could even identify the outcrop near which he was supposed to make his landing.

The pilot flew them the full length of the ridge. At its center he dropped a smoke bomb and circled over its trailing plume of white. The wind was blowing from the south, Hank noted, toward the fire. The pilot and Stemple shouted briefly at each other; then the plane swung onto a course a little south of the ridge.

Now it was past the eastern edge of the smoke cloud. Now it was turning in a great circle. Now the thunder of the engines died to nothing, the plane went into a long, shallow glide, and Stemple was coming toward him. Silently John snapped first Hank's and then Dade's static cord to the wire stretched along the roof of the cabin.

Over the rustle of air on the wing surfaces, Dade's voice was startlingly loud. "I want you to promise me one thing, Stemp. If I freeze in the door, boot me out."

John nodded and Hank followed him to the doorway, watched him undo the fastenings and jerk it open. John's hand steadied him in the gap as he leaned against the air blast, clutching the radio in both arms.

John's voice echoed hollowly inside his mask: "When I tap your shoulder, step off. Good luck, kid."

"Ready to go," Hank shouted back. It seemed to

him that the plane was skimming the very top of the ridge. He had an almost overpowering impulse to draw back and his muscles froze, fighting it. "That's a funny thing," he thought, "Jim's scared." He felt the tap on his shoulder. It released the taut energy locked inside him. In a great, clumsy surge, he dove head-first out of the plane.

"Me too," he cried aloud. Then the parachute jerked him upright so violently that his teeth rattled.

Of that slow descent to earth under his silken canopy which he had dreaded and wondered about so much during the last few hours, Hank never remembered anything. It was a low-altitude jump, so that the wind would not blow him over the clifflike northern face of the ridge and into the arms of the fire. Before he had time to recover fully from the shock of the opening parachute, he was on the ground.

He hit hard but on balance and immediately rolled over and over, curling himself around his radio, as Stemple had shown him. The parachute collapsed partly on top of him. There was a brief, suffocating struggle with its limp folds and then he was his own master again, feet on the earth. He took off mask, parachute harness, equipment belt and finally the jumpsuit. They had served him well and he hated to abandon them to the fire. But he was done with them now, with everything but the belt which carried all his tools and instruments.

This he buckled again around his waist. As he did so his eyes automatically searched along the ridge. He saw the glimmer far off of the wings of the plane and under it he saw something like a great white moth floating. Dade was on his way down. It would be several minutes before he could expect to hear from his companions. Hank stamped up and down restlessly, itching to get on with his task, bending every few seconds over the radio. The instrument stared unwinkingly back at him with the one red eye of the tuning dial and was silent except for the faint frying noise of static.

Just when Hank's nerves screamed at him that they could stand no more, the radio gave a deeper hum and then spoke with Stemple's voice. "Stemple to Winton, Stemple to Winton, Stemple to Winton. Come in, Hank."

Hank flipped the switch to "Transmit" and said, "Winton back. On the ground and all O.K., John. Go ahead."

"That's swell," replied Stemple. "Stand by. Stemple to Dade. Stemple to Dade. Stemple to Dade. Come in, Jim."

There was a pause and John repeated his call before Dade's voice said, "Dade back to Stemple. Not quite so good here, John. I'm hung up in this butterfly net and can't get loose."

"Are you hurt?" asked John. "I'd better come over there."

"Don't do that," Dade shot back. "Get on with the job. I'm all tangled up here like a bronc in a war bridle, but I'm all right. If I don't get loose you can pick me up when you're finished."

Hank wordlessly echoed John's next question: "Well, but what about the fire? Is it near you?"

"Not near enough to worry about. I'll call you if I begin to smoke. Go on now, quit arguing and get busy." Even over the radio, Dade sounded hysterical with rage.

"O.K., Jim, if you say you're all right. Stand by. Stemple to pilot. Stemple to pilot. Come in."

A heavier carrier wave made Hank's tiny receiver vibrate. "Pilot back. Roger on all transmissions. What are you going to do now, Stemple? Go ahead."

"Stemple to pilot, Dade and Winton. Winton and

I will proceed to scout the fire. We'll both work back to pick up Dade. Stand by, pilot, to relay fire information. Acknowledge . . . Dade, open your set every fifteen minutes so you can help us locate you. Acknowledge . . . Winton, use your set only when necessary. These little things are only good for a short while. Acknowledge."

"Pilot to Stemple. Roger and standing by."

"Dade to Stemple. Roger and out."

"Winton to Stemple. Roger and out."

Hank tucked his radio under one arm, took a last look around to make sure of his landmarks, and began to scramble downhill. He was wearing his headlamp but did not turn it on. The moon was bright enough to read by. Soon his lungs recoiled from the sting of smoke. But he plunged on, his caulks alternately gritting on rock and tearing up the pine-needle carpet, inches thick, that covered the forest floor.

He felt the fire before he saw it—a searing wave of heat—then, low down in the smoke, a red glow spreading out to right and left. He went close enough to make sure that the fire was burning slowly along the ground. Now and then a dry bush became a momentary torch as the flames reached hungrily for the canopy of tree branches far overhead. But they always died down again to the sullen glow. The thick-barked tamaracks and spruce of his own Forest, Hank knew, would survive such a fire as this. But not the thin-skinned white pines. All around him, in silent, immovable agony, the thousands of splendid trees were dying.

Hank backed away out of the worst of the heat. He checked his compass. Then, on a line paralleling the front of the fire, he dogtrotted east. Now and then a swirl of clean air penetrated the pall of smoke and his tortured lungs sucked at it greedily. It was impossible to estimate time or distance, but he was coughing, his legs were like putty and he was sick to his stomach when a thinning of the smoke told him that he had reached the flank of the fire. He made sure, ranging several hundred yards into unburned timber and tracing the smoldering edge of the conflagration.

There were no landmarks in the smoke. The broken ground gave him no clue to direction. Even the stars were blotted out. But Hank calmly opened his compass, read its phosphorescent dial and headed due south, back to the ridge. The cool night air soon cut the smoke out of his lungs. Even while traveling rapidly uphill, he began to revive.

On the ridge he spread his map, turned the beam

of his headlamp on it, and began to check his landmarks. When he was sure, he pencilled a dot on the map to show his position and a line to indicate the front of the fire. Then he opened his radio.

"Winton to pilot. Winton to pilot. Come in."

He heard the faraway hum of the plane hovering overhead. "Pilot to Winton. Go ahead," came the voice as if from the stars.

"Winton to pilot. Reporting at 10:31 P.M. The east flank of the fire is in Section 10, Township 1 South of Range 5 East. The fire front is approximately one-quarter mile from the ridge as far west as Section 7, same Township and Range. It is traveling slowly on the ground. Wind is steady from the south. Go ahead."

"Pilot to Stemple. Roger on your message. I will relay. Go ahead."

"Have you heard from Stemple?"

"Yes, he called a few minutes ago. Said he was having trouble. He's got into some very rough country where the fire is all broken up. He expects to be delayed."

"O.K. When he calls again, tell him I've gone to look for Dade and will scout Dade's area on the way. Have you heard from Jim?"

"He's been calling regularly. He's due on again at 10:45."

Hank traveled rapidly along the sparsely timbered ridge. He passed the rocky pinnacle which had been his own jump target, saw the heap of his abandoned equipment. But he did not pause. Whenever the footing was good, he broke into a run. For he was anxious now to get to Jim. Somehow, Dade's tale of his predicament did not ring true. He just could not imagine Dade so tangled up in anything that he couldn't free himself, unless he were hurt.

At 10:45 he opened his set and called. Dade responded instantly.

"Can you give me any idea where you are, Jim?" asked Hank, blessing the marvelous little machine that let them talk as if they were side by side.

"Can't tell you much," replied Jim. "I was all set to touch bottom right on the ridge. Then a gust of wind came along. I sort of glanced off a boulder and came down in the timber on the north side. And here I hang like a Christmas tree ornament. . . . Hurry up, dude, and get me out of this."

Hank grinned. As long as Jim could talk like his insulting self there wasn't too much wrong with him. "What about landmarks?" he asked.

"Well, there's that boulder, sort of a pinto-colored job and plenty big. My jump mark was a tall, dead snag on the ridge but I wasn't paying any attention to it when I landed. That pilot flew over while you were prowling around. Thought he might pick up my parachute, but no luck. Guess that's all I can tell you." All at once Dade sounded infinitely weary.

"All right," said Hank. "That ought to be enough. I'll call you back in fifteen minutes."

But he found dozens of tall dead snags and many a "pinto-colored" boulder, every one of them big. He began to get uneasy. He knew that he must be close, but there was no time to waste, with the fire ceaselessly eating its way toward the trapped smokejumper. The radio was maddening now. It gave no indication of distance and they might be a mile or fifty yards apart.

Along a wide front, Hank roamed the ridge, making little excursions into the timber at likely spots, always coming back disappointed. At last he called Dade and said, "Jim, I don't seem to be getting anywhere. The only thing I can figure is to move along the ridge whooping and hollering. Maybe you'll hear me and then you can tell me on the radio." He was frantic with worry. Dade's voice had been getting steadily weaker, whether because Jim was weakening himself or because his radio was giving out, Hank could not be sure.

"All right," Dade answered. "Anything you say." There was a long pause, although Hank could tell that Jim still had his transmitter turned on. Then the dragging voice spoke again. "Please don't ask me to talk any more . . . I—I——" Then there was silence.

Hank jumped as if something had stung him. Those last words hadn't come out of his radio. He had heard them direct, from under his very feet. He leaned out over the lip of the ridge, a sheer drop of fifty feet at this point. Below him he saw an immense old tree and, hanging in its lower branches, something unnaturally white. Whorls of smoke came up out of the depths to torment his eyes. But he had seen enough.

He found a way around the cliff and scrambled down. In another moment he had reached the tree. There, supported by the shroudlines of the parachute, feet barely off the ground, dangled the figure of Jim Dade. Even in the bulky jump suit, it was plain that one leg and one arm hung at a queer angle and that his head drooped forward limply.

As Hank paused, transfixed by pity and amazement, there was a fierce crackle in the gloom farther down the slope and a brief glare as a bush dissolved in flames.

# T W E L V E

## Crawford's Men

"BEATEN to a pulp, but he wouldn't quit," thought Hank Winton as he looked at the unconscious figure of Jim Dade dangling under his parachute. But amazement and pity occupied only part of his mind. Hank had been well trained. He was first of all a forester in a tight place and his immediate thought was to size up the situation.

With one half of his mind he could admire Jim's superb courage in telling them over the radio that he was all right, to get on with the job; he could feel pity for the pain and fear that Dade had endured through the long hours of waiting. The other half of his mind was as cold and precise as a firefinder. It told him a number of things in one instantaneous flash. It told him that Dade had fallen at the head of a steep and narrow gully, heavily timbered, where all the draft set up by a fire would congregate. It told him that in this open air chimney the fire had advanced far ahead of the general front, that it was ready to blow up and consume everything in a sea of flame.

Hank had every human being's mortal fear of burning. He could smell the stench and hear the eager crackle of it, could feel its hot breath upon his face. His wildly beating heart and his tense nerves urged him to run. Nothing held him here—his legs were strong under him—nothing but the invisible bonds that stretch between companions in danger. In a moment no longer than one heartbeat and without ever realizing it, Hank passed the final test of a forester.

Purposefully now he went into action. One arm went round Dade's flaccid body, supporting it. The other slashed with a knife at the webbing of the parachute. Dade's weight settled upon him, and even in unconsciousness the smokechaser groaned.

There was no time to treat the wounded man's injuries. Out of the gloom the fire was snarling at Hank like a beast. With Dade in his arms, he began his climb back to the temporary safety of the ridge. Almost at once he learned a bitter lesson. He did not have the superhuman strength of the movie hero who carries a wounded companion lightly up interminable battlements. This was reality. In less than a hundred feet his knees buckled and his eyes grew dim while his lungs struggled for oxygen. Neither he nor any other man could carry a full-grown human being up that slope erect.

But there were other ways. Scarcely pausing, Hank wrestled Dade's body onto his back and held him there by his one good arm. Then crawling on hands and knees, yard by yard, foot by foot and finally inch by inch, he fought for both their lives. His steel-shod feet cut long gouges in the loose dirt, left scratches a quarter of an inch deep in solid rock. To every inch of distance gained he clung with elbows, shoulders and fingernails.

The fire reached the spot where Dade's empty parachute trailed its severed cords in the moonlight. Balked of its prey, the fire climbed the tree where Dade had hung, leaping from a huckleberry bush to a festoon of Spanish moss and into the silken folds. The chute blazed momentarily and outlined the whole tree in furious radiance.

A hundred yards away, Hank lay on his face and gasped for breath. Slowly he heaved himself up into traveling position once more and struggled on. The climb was endless. Like some crippled, limbless thing he contracted himself into a ball and then shoved himself upward, measuring the path to escape with his body. Each spasm of motion was slower and more painful than the last.

Eventually his clutching hand reached up into nothingness and then dropped back to the lip of the ridge. There he hung. His legs doubled under him, refusing the frantic urging of his will. Slowly, unwillingly, they began to relax and let him slip back.

Then, as he squirmed there against the face of the cliff, it seemed to him that the dead weight on his back became miraculously lighter. As if of its own volition, Jim's body slid forward and upward. Dazed and sick from exhaustion, only half conscious, Hank felt his burden lift. He was ready to let go now and drop into the waiting arms of the fire. Anything to ease his tortured muscles.

A peremptory voice spoke in his ear: "All right, you next." Strong hands seized him by the collar and dragged him bodily onto the ridge.

Face up in the moonlight he lay while his gaping mouth clutched at the cool air. Physically he was paralyzed, but his senses were working. He heard the mechanical squawk of a radio repeating over and over, "Pilot to Stemple, Pilot to Stemple. I've lost contact with you. What's going on?"

Hank's knotted muscles relaxed when he heard the answer. "Stemple to pilot. It's all right now. We've got Dade and he's badly hurt. If you have contact with the advance party tell them to get on up here with that bulldozer. The fire is about to jump the ridge in one place. We're starting out with Dade now."

"Pilot to Stemple. Roger on your message. I will relay. Do you want me to try a landing on the ridge? Think I could sit down about half a mile west of you."

Hank heard John chuckle to himself, "He would too, crazy bush flyer." Then, "Stemple to pilot. No, thanks a lot, you keep that kite up where it belongs. You can help us most by getting word to that bulldozer crew. Signing off now."

John turned from the radio without waiting for the pilot to acknowledge. The plane flew low up the ridge, engines howling, and then swung away to the south. Hank sat up, feeling slightly dizzy. His movements were slow and awkward, but he was recovering rapidly.

"Oh, so you're going to come out of it, are you?"

remarked Stemple. "Was wondering if I'd have to lug both you jokers out of here." He was already busy over the still figure in the jump suit, talking to himself as he worked: "Got to splint him up a little before we move him. Better leave him right in this snuggle-bunny outfit." Dade groaned again as Stemple gently straightened the twisted limbs and began to bandage them.

Hank rolled over on hands and knees and gave a surprised grunt of pain. In the glow of Stemple's headlamp he discovered that his tough denim pants were torn to ribbons, his hands slippery with blood.

"You ready for business?" demanded John. "Get busy and build us a travois to haul Jim on."

Hank stood up, automatically drying his hands on his shirt. "Travois?" he faltered.

"Yeah. You know, like the Indians use to drag their stuff behind a horse. Only make it smaller, man-size. One of us will have to pull it while the other cuts trail. And get going. This place isn't healthy."

As if to emphasize his words, a great banner of flame leaped high above the ridge. The south wind blew it back, away from them, but its heat was momentarily unbearable. A rain of cinders fell on them, stinging every inch of exposed flesh.

Hank knew what John wanted now. He freed his light axe from its scabbard and cut two slim poles. He laid them down on the ground, their points almost touching at one end, several feet apart at the other. Shorter poles laid crosswise made the platform on which Dade would lie. His jump-rope provided the lashings. In a few minutes Stemple joined him and they finished the job in wordless teamwork.

Carefully then they laid Jim on the platform and tied him in place. It was an ingenious contrivance, for now less than half Dade's weight lay on the shoulders of the man pulling the travois. Most of it was supported by the poles which could slide easily along the ground. Only a woodsman could have thought of it in that desperate hour.

"How is he?" asked Hank. "We've got to save him. He's the bravest guy alive."

Stemple gave him a peculiar look and opened his mouth to say something, then seemed to change his mind. After the moment's hesitation, he said, "Yeah. He did all right, didn't he? He's got two bad fractures, but shock is the worst thing. Let's scram out of here before those spot fires link up and corral us. I'll take the first hitch on the go-devil. You cut trail. Head straight south and keep to the high ground."

He got between the shafts of the travois and adjusted the shoulder harness he had made of the two jump belts.

While they had been working, sparks from the inferno under the ridge had flown over and landed on the southern slope. Each one was now a spreading pool of crimson. Hank threaded a way past this barrier, pausing now and again to slash at the thicket of young jackpines and tear an opening in their ranks wide enough for the travois. His hands seemed to be on fire and his whole body ached, but he ignored their protests. In his wake, Stemple plodded steadily forward.

Time went by, measured not in minutes but in weary yards. The moon went down and they traveled in inky darkness which seemed to muffle their headlamps. Behind them, from time to time, a clump of the explosive little trees would ignite one after the other like a fireworks display and tatter the velvet darkness. Then, imperceptibly, the night began to fade.

In the gray light of false dawn, Hank and Stemple moved like automatons. Occasionally they traded places. They never spoke now. They were beyond words, almost beyond thought and feeling. They stumbled on because they had forgotten how to stop. Neither of them was conscious of a faint mechanical roar which grew louder as the minutes passed. They stared in dull astonishment when, a hundred feet ahead of them, the hedge of jackpines suddenly trembled and then toppled over toward them.

In the gap appeared a huge caterpillar tractor. Its treads clanked to a halt and from the broad swath left by its blade men swarmed out to surround the fugitives. A babble of questions drummed in their ears. But Hank and John merely swung their heads from one face to another, unable to answer.

A voice they recognized cut through the din: "All right, break it up and let the doc through," said Supervisor Hardy. "The six of you right there drop off to help get these boys to the road. Up the mountain with the rest of you."

The tractor swung on its treads and passed the little group around the travois; the fire crew filed by and disappeared with many a curious backward look. Beside Dade a man in dusty city clothes opened a black satchel. Almost as if on signal Hank and John sat down in the middle of the wide, raw trail of the bulldozer.

They accepted water from Hardy and nibbled

hungrily on bars of chocolate. Patiently the Supervisor waited until they could recover a little. "So you did it?" he said at last. "Believe me, this night's work will go on a page by itself. We're throwing in everything we've got on the basis of your reports. In another hour there'll be a thousand men and four bulldozers in here. I thought you'd like to know."

"The fire's over the ridge in one place," replied Stemple. "Doesn't amount to much yet. That dozer can push the whole business back over the rim. It's good country for machines. Get 'em up there and you'll hold it."

"Right," said Hardy. "I'll leave you to the doctor. I'm releasing you to your own Forest. When you see Crawford tell him thanks and if the Sacajawea can ever do anything for him to let us know." He hurried up the trail.

The doctor came over saying, "I can't improve much on your first-aid job. Let's have a look at you two. Drink this." He handed each of them a cup of milky fluid.

Hank smelt the sweetish, stinging odor of aromatic spirits of ammonia. "Seems to me I practically live on this stuff," he said, wrinkling his nose as he swallowed.

"How's Dade?" coughed Stemple.

"Your partner? Well, he's got a long rest in the hospital ahead of him with those fractures. He's in shock badly enough to kill an ordinary man, but he'll make it. You're all being flown to Midvale as soon as we get you out of here. Feel up to traveling another mile or two?"

Unheeded, another man in city clothes had been listening and writing feverishly on a wad of yellow paper. No one paid him any attention or even heard the click as he aimed a camera at the group. He had already disappeared down the trail at a dog trot when Hank and Stemple got clumsily to their feet. The little procession started downhill, Hank and John in the lead and each being supported by two men. Two men followed carrying Dade on the travois, and the doctor brought up the rear.

Hank and John were glad to stumble along between their helpers. The doctor had spread a soothing ointment on Hank's hands and bandaged them. They were mercifully numb now and he had an overpowering desire to sleep. Soon after the procession started it seemed to him that he heard the shuffle of many feet, the murmur of many voices, the roaring of powerful machines. But he did not raise his head, even when some of the words he heard were plain: "Who're those guys? . . . Smokejumpers. Scouted the fire. . . . They're sure beat up. . . . They can have my share of that racket. . . . Where're they from? . . . Three Rivers. Jack Crawford's men. . . . Oh."

It became a sort of refrain: "Three Rivers . . . Crawford's men. . . . Three Rivers . . . Crawford's men . . . Three Rivers Crawford's men. . . . Threeriverscrawfordsmen."

He was vaguely conscious of a short, bumpy ride in an automobile. He knew when he was helped into a plane and deposited on the delightful softness of a sleeping bag. Then, at last, he slept.

He woke to find John shaking him and saying, "Roll out, firefighter. We're in town. Which will you have first, meal or bath?"

"Bath," replied Hank instantly, although his mouth watered at the mere mention of food. His whole body felt sticky and uncomfortable from the mixture of sweat, dust and soot which had dried on it. He was stiff and sore in every muscle, as though he had been beaten with hammers. "I bet I smell bad, and you look as if you'd been pulled through a chimney."

"Look who's talking," retorted Stemple. "Wonder what the mob is doing at the airport. Some big shot must be coming in."

Hank hoisted himself up to look but the first thing he saw was an ambulance backing up to the plane. The cabin door opened and white-coated attendants lifted Dade onto a stretcher while an interne directed every move. Dade was still muffled in his jump suit and still wearing the crude splints John had applied in the light from the fire. It seemed impossible now that only a few hours ago they had been struggling for their lives in the heart of a flame-swept wilderness.

The ambulance drove away and uncovered a solid phalanx of people. Hank said, "Well, anyway, I see Crawford and my dad out there."

"And the Regional Forester and the Fire Chief and enough more brass to fill a hall," added Stemple. "Let's go get that bath before his Nibs arrives, whoever he is."

John no sooner appeared in the open door of the plane than a woman's high-pitched voice screamed, "There they are—the smokejumpers."

Stemple retreated into the cabin. "What is this?" he demanded.

The sight of him backing up from a mere crowd of

people filled Hank with a hysterical desire to giggle. Crawford's face, wearing its usual ironic smile, framed itself in the doorway. "You might as well come out and take it," he drawled. "You would go and be heroes."

# T H I R T E E N

## The Real Reunion

IN THE brief period since the man with the camera and the wad of yellow paper had run down the trail ahead of Hank and John, a good many things had happened. Telephone and telegraph had been busy. Newspaper presses had rumbled to a stop and then turned again at full speed. During the first hour of their airplane trip to Midvale a man in a soundproof booth had shuffled his hastily scribbled notes and turned to his microphone.

"Ladies and gentlemen of the radio audience," he had said, "this is your radio reporter with the first newscast of the day. All across the world many things have happened during the night. But for us who live in the mountains there is only one story this morning. I'm going to tell it to you in full.

"Last night, while nations snarled at each other over an acre or two of land, while financiers squabbled over profits and politicians over power, while gamblers cheated and thieves stole, last night three young men risked their lives in a purely unselfish cause.

"At ten o'clock they parachuted into the path of the monster forest fire which has been burning out of control for days in the Sacajawea National Forest. Their purpose was to scout the fire and prepare the way for the army of firefighters coming in this morning to try to halt the conflagration.

"Two of them landed safely and went about their ticklish business. From their radio reports came the information that has sent a thousand firefighters and four tractors into the wilderness with an excellent chance of halting the blaze. But the third parachutist was caught by a gust of wind just as he was landing. He was slammed against a boulder, breaking one arm and one leg, and then blown over a cliff. At the bottom, his parachute lodged in a tree and left him dangling helplessly in the path of the fire. Yet this boy, he's only nineteen, had the incredible fortitude to radio his companions that he was not hurt and in no danger.

"Eventually the others, with their dangerous task

finished, came to look for him. One of them found him when the fire was only a few yards away. He cut the chutist free and with the fire at his heels carried him up the almost perpendicular cliff. I'm not reading this out of a book, radio listeners. This actually happened only a few hours ago. The third smoke-jumper arrived in time to drag them both practically out of the fire.

"This was only the beginning of their ordeal. They were still miles away from any help and the fire was getting ready to blow up, as the foresters say. So the two uninjured smokejumpers calmly set about giving first aid to their companion. Then, with one of them cutting trail and the other dragging the injured man on an improvised travois, they began their race with the fire.

"It was a queer sort of race, measured in yards, not miles per hour. It went on all the rest of the night. At six o'clock this morning, when they met a rescue party equipped with a bulldozer, they had traveled— would you like to guess, people of the Air Age? After half a night of heartbreaking toil, they had gained just about a mile.

"Your morning paper will have a photograph of

them, taken where they met the rescue party. Look at their faces and see what it cost them to save the timber for our houses, the water for our rivers, our favorite fishing streams and camping grounds. You may even see them in person, for they are being flown to the hospital in Midvale at this moment.

"Their names? One you ought to recognize: John Stemple, alternate ranger of the Three Rivers District of our own Evergreen National Forest, leader of the party. Second is Henry Winton, son of a United States senator, serving his first year as a forest fire lookout. And the third, the one who was so badly injured, is James Dade, also a lookout and a native of this city. Winton and Dade, believe this or not, jumped without previous parachute training. There's only one word that fits such men—they're heroes."

This story, told with all the skill and emotion of a practised raconteur, had winged into thousands of homes. Loudspeakers had blared it along the streets. It had stirred the hearts of people who could look up from their little yards to the limitless grandeur of the wilderness. It had brought them to the airport; it held them in deep and silent ranks around the hospital, and a dozen heads craned over each copy of the newspaper extra with its banner headline:

## SMOKEJUMPERS ESCAPE FIRE

Hank had a copy of that extra, laid in his bandaged hands by his father. He had glanced at it from time to time during their ride to Crawford's house through the crowded streets of Midvale. But he looked without seeing the printed words. Everything that had happened since he woke up in the plane seemed to him unreal and impossible. He was glad when they reached the quiet and shelter of the ranger's home.

Only one thing made any impression on him: the photograph in the paper. Could those two wretched creatures with tattered clothes and soot-smeared faces be himself and John? Heroes? He began to laugh and the world fell into normal focus again.

He and John had their baths, in oceans of steaming water. Fresh clothes for them appeared as if by magic, or possibly as the result of a short disappearance by the ranger and Senator Winton. They ate an enormous meal, with Dorothy and Mrs. Crawford hovering over them to refill their plates before they were even emptied.

But through all Hank's enjoyment of the comforts he and John had dreamed about there ran a somber thread. A half-formed thought had nagged at him ever since the moment he knew Dade was hurt. Now it was taking shape.

As John and the ranger left the dining room, Hank's father laid a hand on his arm. "For a hero who has just been bathed, clothed and stuffed, who has his picture in all the papers and his name on the radio, you seem uncommon gloomy," said the Senator. "What's on your mind, son?"

Hank looked into the sharp, understanding eyes and blurted, "Jim Dade. What's to become of him now?"

Senator Winton, who could not possibly know what his son was talking about, did not let that appear in voice or manner. He said, "Crawford and John are going to Regional Headquarters. They want John to dictate a report on this little shindy you boys pulled off. I don't see why you and I shouldn't take a run over to the hospital and see Dade. Those dressings on your hands should be changed anyway."

Whatever a father's heart may have felt about those hands muffled in gauze, this was the only reference the Senator had made to them. With his usual exquisite tact, he realized that Hank was embarrassed by his injuries, minor in comparison to what Dade had suffered. He had been stared at and pitied and exclaimed over until all he wanted was to be left alone.

Hank brightened at the idea of seeing Dade. They set out and with a few casual questions on the way, the Senator extracted the story of Jim Dade.

"He and I worked together a few weeks before we went up on our towers," Hank explained. "I couldn't make the guy out at all. He seemed to have it in for me and I couldn't figure out why because we'd never seen each other before. We got into some fights and boy did he whale the stuffing out of me."

"He, whale the stuffing out of you? Why, you're a third again his size," objected the Senator.

"Yeah, but he's a professional boxer. Anyhow, it came out little by little what the trouble was. He didn't know me but he knew who I was from last summer. He figured me for a playboy, riding on your shirt tail and aiming at something he's had to fight for every inch of the way. And fight is just what I mean. He's earned the money for his education and everything he has with his fists. That's really something, isn't it?"

"Unusual determination, to say the least," agreed his father.

"The only thing that can stop a guy like that is to get smashed up. And there you are. What becomes of him now?"

"Well, but doesn't the Forest Service take care of its casualties? After all——"

"You don't understand, Dad. Sure, Uncle will see him through the hospital. But what about his education? It will be a long time before he can pay a tuition bill again with his gloves. And this forestry is a tough proposition. You can't afford to lose a year. The show has to go on and there are too many guys looking for your place."

The Senator nodded his understanding. "Yes, I see the problem now. Let me think about it a bit. Tell me, do you like Dade?"

"Like him?" Hank pondered the question while his thoughts went back over the events of the fire season: his meeting with Dade at Puzzle Basin, working with him on the trails, arguing with him over their smokechasers' bibles; their first fight when Dade couldn't bring himself to land the finishing blow; Dade calling him a lucky stiff because he'd drawn a tough fire, bluffing the mob after his fight with the logger; Dade telling Stemple to boot him out of the plane if he froze when the moment came to jump.

Somehow, that was the most human touch of all.

"He's the hardest guy to get along with, the most cross-grained and ornery critter that ever lived," said Hank finally. "But yes, I like him."

At the hospital a doctor immediately whisked Hank into a room and deftly cut off his bandages. Even Hank was surprised when he saw the deep cuts and gouges and the nails torn off deep into the quick.

"Good," said the doctor cheerfully as he worked. "No infection. Should be all healed up in a few weeks. You foresters play kind of rough, don't you?" He finished tying the new bandages. "You'll find your buddy in the second room down the hall."

Hank was ill at ease when he stood at last at Dade's bedside. After an introduction and a few words, his father had tactfully disappeared. Hank got over the awkward moment with a joking, "Thought you were pretty well hog-tied in that parachute but this is really fancy." He referred to the traction bed in which Jim lay with his arm and leg supported by a maze of ropes, pulleys and weights.

Dade could move nothing but his eyes, but they snapped with the familiar fire and it was the same old Jim who snarled, "You don't look so good yourself, dude. What about that stinking fire? Around here every time I open my mouth to ask, some jerk shoves either a thermometer or a pill into it."

"We got a report half an hour ago. It's under control. They stopped it along the ridge."

"Well, that's something." Dade looked away for a moment and when he spoke again his voice was unsteady. "I might as well get this over with. I'm taking back a lot of things I said and thought about you— Hank. Silver spoon, politics, iron in the soul and all that kid stuff. I don't know how one guy could be such a dope."

"Aw, skip it," begged Hank in an agony of embarrassment for himself and Dade both. "I had it coming to me."

"Well, I suppose you'll be going back to the district. Wonder who they'll put on Minaret?" And now Jim's voice was full of hopeless longing.

"We're flying in tomorrow, I think," said Hank. "I'll let you know how things go and I'll see you again as soon as the season's over."

"Do that and I'll be seeing you, Hank."

On the way back to Crawford's house the Senator said, "Quite an unusual personality, your friend Dade. As for that problem, it wasn't so difficult after all. I don't know why it took so long for me to remember that there's a scholarship in Forestry at your own college. As a member of the Board of Trustees I think I could get it awarded to Jim. Would you like that?"

Hank looked at his father with a knowing grin. "Pop," he said, "I'd bet you my summer's pay that scholarship got established about five minutes ago." And then more seriously, "It's swell of you—but it wouldn't work. Not with Dade. He'd see through it quicker than I did and probably tell you to go fly a kite."

"Yes, I assumed as much," replied his father drily. "But you see, this scholarship will be offered through the Forest Service, as compensation for injuries received in the course of duty. It's a new policy, just adopted by the Service."

Finally at peace in body, mind and conscience, Hank settled back.

At the ranger's house they found Stemple and Crawford. "We were just discussing you," said the latter. "You'll be handicapped for a while with those muslin boxing mitts. Thought we'd transfer you to district headquarters for the rest of the season."

"Do you have to?" asked Hank unhappily. "I know I could run the firefinder and keep the records. I'd rather go back to my tower."

"But Hank, you couldn't cook and haul water and things like that," protested Dorothy.

Hank wondered why John and the ranger were grinning at each other so delightedly.

"I have a possible solution," the Senator put in. "If regulations permit, I'd like to volunteer as assistant lookout, do the cooking and the chores and so on."

The ranger appeared to study this offer judicially while his mouth twitched uncontrollably at the corners. "We'd certainly prefer to keep an experienced lookout on Sliderock," he admitted. "Two lookouts for the price of one . . . the Debating Society has been after us every day to know when Sliderock was going on the air again . . . It's a deal."

Something clicked in Hank's mind. A month ago this conversation could never have taken place. It could now because at last he belonged. Though he felt no different inside, there was a difference in everything around him. He was at home, a forester among others of his kind, and this was the real reunion.